BAT OUT OF HELL

BERNADETTE FRANKLIN

BAT OUT OF HELL
BY BERNADETTE FRANKLIN

After shredding a Prada for a costume, Shirley Manchester fears she opened a portal to hell. With a fashion designer out for revenge hot on her heels, a secret admirer on a mission to evict her from the pool of eligible bachelorettes, and a relentless streak of bad luck, surviving through Halloween is turning into a sketchy proposition.

Next time, Shirley will remember there are better ways to dodge an unwanted advance than kissing a random stranger.

Escaping the party turns out to be only the beginning of Shirley's woes. Curses aren't supposed to be real, but after the going keeps getting tougher, she's at real risk of becoming a believer in the things that go bump in the night.

The tricks should've ended in October, but her November is looking to be one hell of a wild ride.

ONE

Booh, the favorite of my felt bat monstrosities, lived on my shoulder

IN THE CREATIVITY DEPARTMENT, I scored a zero on my Halloween costume. I blamed Clarissa; if she'd given me more than three days' notice I needed to go to a Halloween party with her, I would've been able to dress up as something better than a gothic witch with an unhealthy interest in bats and crystals. I should've gotten some fake teeth and gone the vampire route, but the damage was already done.

Booh, the favorite of my felt bat monstrosities, lived on my shoulder, permanently attached to my dress.

The dress would rise from the dead later and haunt me, of that I was sure. In a complete lapse of sanity, I'd butchered my Prada, a slinky black dress I'd saved for two years to buy, and I slapped on a belt which I'd decorated with clear quartz spears I'd acquired from a New Age shop. With a little luck, they'd offer sanctuary from the inevitable surge of creepers I'd meet at the party. Then, as I'd already slaughtered my self-respect, I raided my closet for my black shoes and only pair of fishnet stockings, which I doubted would survive the night.

To add insult to injury, I wasn't even sure why I bothered with the stockings; they were barely visible beneath the tattered ends of my abused dress.

Next time, I'd leave my dignity at the door and buy one of the slutty witch costumes from a pop-up store rather than ruin my only nice dress for the sake of a friend.

Clarissa owed me, but damn it, I was too nice to call her out on it. Miss Money Bags might recognize the Prada for what it was, but she likely wouldn't think twice about it. She owned a zillion of them and wouldn't miss one if it vanished from her closet. My jealousy surged, and I shook my head at my pettiness.

It wasn't Clarissa's fault that her father was a banker, and her mother was a movie star with more money than any god. It puzzled me the family didn't live in California, instead choosing New Jersey as their stomping grounds of choice.

I still wasn't sure how I'd become friends with the woman, but it was her fault I'd saved up for my Prada, and it was definitely her fault I'd lost my mind and trashed it.

Reality smacked me between the eyes and left me with a skull splitter of a headache, the kind that'd leave me wanting to throw up the entire night.

Right. I'd used my Prada because the party was taking place at a posh penthouse in the heart of Manhattan, where the attendees rolled in cash and likely bathed in it before bed each night. I'd gotten an invitation on the grounds of being a good, grounding influence on Clarissa, whatever the hell that meant. During the week, I worked at an upscale boutique while pretending I could afford the kind of clothes

I sold. Saturdays, I washed dishes at an equally upscale restaurant.

Neither job qualified me to be a good, grounding influence.

And nothing qualified me to go to a damned Halloween party for the rich and famous, but according to my phone, I had no more than ten minutes before a limo arrived to cart me off to the most humiliating night of my life.

Why couldn't I have told Clarissa no?

Oh, right. I had exactly three friends, and Clarissa was one of them. Sophia and Lily were more Clarissa's friends than mine, but they tolerated my presence with grace.

My phone rang, and the display informed me Clarissa wished to grace me with her stunning intellect and charm. Already regretting every decision in my life leading up to this moment, I answered, "Hello, Clarissa."

"You sound less than thrilled to be coming to the hottest Halloween party in New York, Shirley."

No matter what I did, I couldn't escape my name. One day, I would pay the government to change it to something better. Anything other than Shirley. "Couldn't you just call me Lee? Please? I'll beg."

"But then I sound like I'm talking to a boy, and you're no boy."

"I'm fine with this. I would rather be a boy named Lee than a girl named Shirley. This is proof my mother hated me from birth."

"Your mother adores you, and we both know it. Don't make me call your mom and make her cry. She will, too."

My mother really would, and I'd never hear the end of it. It would lead to darkness and a family dinner my mother insisted Clarissa would have to attend, and if Clarissa got her way, her parents would attend, too. The disasters would be as plentiful as the food.

My mother could charm the devil with her cooking, and she'd already won over Clarissa's entire family. It'd taken only once for my mother to earn the love of Clarissa's entire family.

Clarissa often searched for excuses for my mother to host a family dinner.

"You are not worming your way into Thanksgiving dinner this year," I announced, acknowledging I lied even as I spoke the words. Without fail, her entire family would be over for the holidays. "You will not seduce my mother again with your sad sighs."

"Already have an invitation for the whole family." Clarissa cackled. "You're just going to have to deal with it, babe."

"I shredded my Prada for you, and I may never forgive you for this. Why am I coming to this thing again?"

"My parents love you; that's why. My mother yelled at me last week for not being born a man. Had I been born a man, I could've married you and made her dreams of having the perfect daughter-in-law come true. She then asked if we were either lesbians or bisexuals. She would've accepted pansexual, too, if she got to have you for a daughter-in-law."

"Don't you have brothers, Clarissa?" Clarissa had three brothers: one a year older than her, one a year younger than her, and one two years younger than her. "Don't encourage your mother. You have brothers."

"My mother has informed them that they are not good enough for you. She's dressing up as Babe Ruth this year just so she can walk around with a baseball bat should they get any ideas."

How had my life become so surreal? I, a poorer-than-dirt

New Jersey denizen, had zero business brushing elbows with the rich and famous or being considered a grand prize future daughter-in-law. "Please explain to me how this happened."

"Well, it started yesterday, actually."

"Just yesterday?"

"This specific incident started just yesterday. It's your own damned fault you're so nice. So, shush and let me tell you a story. The driver should be there in a few minutes. You *are* ready, right? Also, I changed the plans. You're coming with me because my idiot brother changed his mind about attending, and we didn't have enough vehicles. Your limo went to said idiot brother, so we're sharing. In exchange, we have booze for the ride. Mom handed over a half bottle of sparkly to fortify us. It's out of control. The party is actually taking place over the entire top floor now; the neighbors all decided they'd pitch in and host. It's going to be insane."

"Can I refuse to come?"

"No. We're almost to your house. Get your ass outside so we're not clogging up the alley that's stupidly registered as a street. I don't want the limo's wheels stolen. If we sit here for more than five minutes, our wheels will be stolen. This is a fact. I need you to move out of this hellhole immediately if not sooner."

"The rent is cheap, and I shredded my Prada for this event. Now I no longer have a Prada, but my rent will still be cheap."

"You can move in with me. Mother would love if there were a responsible human being keeping an eye on me. According to her, I need to marry a good, responsible man who can rein in my insanity."

"Does such a man even exist?"

"Apparently, he exists, but he was born a woman named Shirley."

Clarissa's mother needed help, and I knew a few psychiatrists, thanks to my father. "So, remember my dad?"

"How could I forget? He was a nutcase, but he was the nicest nutcase in Jersey. Even Mom and Dad miss him and that's saying a lot. He was colorful, but he was cool."

I missed my father despite everything, including the early onset dementia that had claimed his life. The diagnosis had terrified my mother, and when Clarissa's mother had learned about it, she'd offered to pay for my DNA testing herself. Fortunately for my pride, my insurance company had been willing to cover the test.

I'd tested negative for the syndrome, though I do carry the gene responsible for my father's demise. "I know his doctor, and I'm sure he'd be happy to schedule your mother in for an evaluation. I can even put her in touch with my insurance company since they'll foot the bill for DNA testing."

"I still can't believe you gave my mother a copy of your DNA testing results. She forced us to get tested to make sure we didn't have the gene, too. For the record, we don't. She did find out we're predisposed for six types of cancers, so we're being screened yearly now. Failure to show up for our scheduled screenings results in a spanking. I only know this because Damian attempted to skip his screening this year. Dad gave him a spanking."

I decided to ignore the idea that Clarissa's father had given her older brother a spanking. Ignoring the problem might make it go away, so I replied, "It was something I could do for myself, so I did it."

"For the record? That right there is why my mother has a

crush on you. If you hadn't been so damned self-reliant, she wouldn't be crushing all over you right now. You only have yourself to blame for this."

As there was no escaping Clarissa on a mission, I grabbed the drawstring pouch serving as my purse, tied it to my belt, and headed out of my apartment, triple-checking I locked the door behind me. "Also, just for the record, if you 'for the record' me one more time, I'm inserting my heel directly into your ass. And, you need an appointment with my father's doctor, too."

"Oh, I know I'm crazy. I don't need some damned old man with a PhD to tell me that. I just wanted you to be aware the party is bigger than initially anticipated. It will be chaotic. Please don't insert your shoe in my ass. It takes forever to get one of your shoes out, and I'd rather not need surgical assistance with that task."

"You know my terms, Clarissa."

My friend spat a few curses, hesitated, and cursed some more. "This is cruel and unusual punishment. We're pulling up now."

I trudged down the steps, shoved through the rusting gate responsible for keeping the riff-raff out of the building, and shook my head at the monster of a stretch limo, which had started its life as an SUV. I waited for the vehicle to come to a halt before letting myself in. A giant, inflatable t-rex waved at me.

I closed my door, buckled up, and slapped my head. "The sparkly was a lie, wasn't it?"

"Underneath this t-rex costume, I'm dressed up as a hooker vampire. I just wanted to make a spectacular entrance, and nothing screams a spectacular entrance more than a t-rex emerging from a limo at the hottest party in town carrying a flute of Champagne. You can carry a flute of Champagne, too. I brought two." Clarissa lifted her foot and showed off her heels. "We're Prada girls today. Also, I can't believe you did that to your Prada. That's just insane. My mother is going to see what you've done, and the first thing she's going to do is hunt for her designer friend to show you off. We'll have a betting pool over her friend's reaction. It's going to be priceless, no matter what happens. There's just some things you don't do to a designer dress. This is one of them, Shirley."

"I didn't have any other black dresses."

"You could've been a happy white witch of happiness, summoning cheer to all who meet you. It would've been amazing. Also, your belt is stunning. Actually, your entire outfit is stunning. I want to be you if I ever decide to grow up. And my mother's right. There's no way in hell my brothers are good enough for you."

I couldn't see my friend's face, but I could imagine her expression, which involved a whole lot of cunning married to a splash of evil. "I don't know what you're planning, but the answer is no."

"I have to protect you from my brothers, so I must find a suitable bachelor for you. Though, with you looking like that, you're going to have an entire herd of admirers. You might even bag yourself a *secret* admirer. Do you know what happens when you bag yourself a rich secret admirer?"

"I don't want to know. Rich men tend to forget boundaries and indulge in excess. It would be a disaster."

"But it would be a disaster presented in a Tiffany box."

"Why would a secret admirer use a Tiffany box?"

"That blue box is how rich men try to convince the new love of their life they're really interested."

"Uh huh." I shook my head and poked around the interior of the limo until I located the bottle of Champagne and the promised pair of flutes. As warned, it was a small bottle, and there'd barely be enough for half a glass each. "Please tell me this party will have alcohol."

"A glass a person limit. We're not totally dry, but we're doing one toast only, and that's it."

"You're crushing my dreams of rich people parties being drunken revelries, Clarissa."

"There are a lot of people who don't drink a lot, plus it's a work night. There will also be a bunch of kids around, so we're going the safe route. One day, I'll bring you to one of the drunken revelries. I'm sorry to crush your dreams of having a dalliance with a hot rich guy at a packed party while shit-faced drunk. Maybe next time."

Why was I friends with Clarissa? When I thought about it, it was rather obvious: she made life fun and interesting. "I could have a dalliance with a hot rich guy while sober."

"You could. It would be hot, too—and public. While the penthouses are pretty spacious, there won't be a lot of privacy. Public's not your style, babe."

"Damn. Why am I coming to this party again?"

"You love me."

I did. "Before you showed up dressed like a t-rex, I thought I was too nice of a person to shove this in your face, but you so owe me for this—and you need to replace my Prada. I will take you for every penny of my new Prada, Clarissa. Mark my words."

"How about a Carter dress? You'd rock a Carter."

Sometimes, I worried for my friend's sanity. "If I have to save for two years for a Prada, what makes you think I can afford a Carter?"

"Why are you using logic against someone dressed in an inflatable t-rex costume?"

"Because I'm an idiot."

Clarissa sighed. "If you can afford a Prada, you can afford a Carter. Sure, you can't afford one of the custom Carters, but you can afford a Carter. Some of the outfits are actually cheaper than your Prada. Also, I can't believe you took scissors to your Prada. Also, I'm astonished how good the Prada looks after you helped it to an early grave."

"Witch costumes have tattered dress hems. My Prada didn't have a tattered hem. It needed all the help it could get."

"The accessories are a really nice touch. I'm surprised. You went all in."

"I figured I couldn't have gotten away with going to a pop-up store and slutting it up."

"You totally could have gotten away with going to a pop-up store and slutting it up. Hell, most of us are going to be slutting it up because we can. You will wish this wasn't the case by the time we're done. I'm pretty sure my mother is going as a Baywatch girl if she doesn't show up as Babe Ruth."

"Those swimsuits had a surprising amount of coverage."

"And Mom has the cleavage to turn the swimsuit into something terrifyingly scandalous. I'm just glad I'm no longer embarrassed by anything my mother does."

"It's hard for you to get embarrassed when you're shameless, Clarissa. And don't even bother trying to deny it. You plan on strutting into a Halloween party in an inflatable t-rex costume while holding a flute of Champagne." I checked the bottle. "Pardon, sparkling wine, as it seems you went on the cheap and didn't get any actual Champagne."

"Harsh. What did I do to you?"

"You made me come to this party. Let's start with that. Then, fool that I am, I shredded the only nice piece of clothing I have to come to this party."

"We're a match made in heaven. Why aren't we lesbians?"

I snorted at that. "We like men too much."

In my case, I liked looking at men too much, as I didn't have the time or space in my life for a man. But damn, some days, I wish I did. Cheap thrills only went so far, and nothing ruined my day quite like kicking an ass out of bed before things got good because he had no idea how to play it safe even if I smacked him with a manual and provided the condoms.

"Life is unfair. Why do men have to be so hot when they take their shirts off?"

"Good question."

"Well, in the worst-case scenario, we should get some good eye candy tonight. I hear Tarzan is currently in fashion."

I could imagine so many ways a Tarzan trend could sour in a hurry. "But will the attending men be lazy rich men or frequent flyers of the gym?"

"We'll find out soon enough."

I whimpered. "Can I go home now?"

"Oh, no. Absolutely not, Shirley. The fun has just begun."

For some reason, I doubted even heaven could help me at this point. All I could do was surrender and hope for the best.

"I AM the idiot ruling over all idiots," I announced, eyeballing the bottle of sparkling wine taunting me from its bucket of ice. The alcohol would take the edge off of dealing with Manhattan traffic on Halloween. A ridiculous number of limousines added to the typical New York congestion. Pointing at the window, I waited for Clarissa to figure out the problem.

"They're probably all headed to the same place we are."

"It might be faster to walk."

Clarissa snorted and lifted her leg to show off her pointy stilettos. "In these shoes?"

My shoes weren't much better. "We could take them off and walk barefoot."

"In Manhattan on Halloween? You need to have your head examined. Also, you're full of complaints tonight. We're going to a party. It won't kill you to have some fun, I promise."

"I think we have dramatically different opinions on what counts as fun, Clarissa. I've heard about rich people parties. They're excessive, and everyone judges everyone else by who they're with, how much money they make, who they talk to, or who they've screwed. By bringing me to this party, you will be ranked as the lowest of the low. Then, since that's bad enough, the pecking order is also based on how much money one has to spend on things. You're more like the ruling class on that one, but my presence still dumps you to the back of the pack. Prove I'm wrong. I'm going to be on the absolute last rung because you're probably the only person crazy enough to bring your destitute Jersey friend to a Manhattan penthouse party." Being surly all night long would ruin everyone's fun, mine most of all, so I drew in a deep, cleansing breath. "My Prada might haunt you from its grave. I'm just warning you this is probable."

"You don't even believe in ghosts, witches, or anything that might classify as supernatural."

"I do for tonight only."

"I can work with that as long as you aren't haunting me from your grave. I don't want you to die."

"The Prada is probably coming for me first, so you're going to get a double dose of hauntings."

"That does not sound like a good way to go. I'm too beautiful to be murdered by the vengeful ghosts of my friend and her dress."

"But at least you'd be haunted by a Prada? You could be haunted by a floating white sheet."

"As I have standards, I'm forced to agree with you. You're nervous. It's just a party, Shirley."

"Lee. Please. Spare me from the indignity of calling me Shirley to people. Lee. Just Lee. And text your mother that she's to call me Lee. Then, once this is over, the crazy rich people attending the party won't be able to find me."

"All they'd have to do to find you is ask us for your address."

"You could refuse to tell them. And anyway, there's no 'them.' No one would actually be interested in finding me after this party."

"I beg to differ. You're a hot witch, you have a badass hat, and those crystals on your belt were a stroke of genius. You even have a little fake bat on your shoulder."

"That's my witch's familiar. His name is Booh."

"Booh?"

"Bat out of hell. Booh. He's my spirit animal, as I'd like to run like a bat out of hell right now. I do not belong among a bunch of rich people at a costume party."

"Your spirit animal is made of felt."

"I never said Booh was a good spirit animal."

"Do the other bats have names?"

"No. They're so poorly made their spirits fled to the next life to avoid the shame of being attached to my costume. Only Booh's spirit survived the ordeal of his creation."

"He's made of felt. He doesn't have a soul."

"This is why you will be haunted by my Prada *and* Booh, the Bat."

"Bat out of Hell, the Bat?"

"When you say it like that, my choice of names for my spirit animal is truly unfortunate."

Clarissa cracked up laughing. "I think you're going to be weirder than every other attendee combined. I'm not even sure my mother at her worst can top you and your Booh."

"Go big or go home, and if I'm going to do this, I may as well embrace the insanity. But I'm not responsible for what I'll do if some lecher makes passes at me."

"Some lecher will definitely make passes at you, Shirley."

"Lee, please. Please, Clarissa. I'm begging you. Tonight, call me Lee."

"But I don't want my best girlfriend to be my best boyfriend. I don't want to introduce possible boyfriends to my other boyfriend."

"You can have male friends without dating them."

"You're not a man. We've established this. My mother is very disappointed you're not a man, too. Or that we're not lesbians."

"I do like men too much when they're not assholes. We'll just have to tell your mother we're sorry we haven't succumbed to her plans to transform us into lesbians and marry us off."

"We could adopt you. Then she could have you as a daughter. That would make her happy."

"She would have to sign a co-parenting agreement with my mother." After a moment of consideration, I realized my mother would probably agree to such a thing. "Don't actually suggest that to your mother. My mother would. Yours would leave the party to make sure it was done immediately. I've met your mother. She doesn't let anything sit long."

"Procrastination leads to nothing but trouble in her world."

"Her world is also inhabited by egotistical male asshole producers and actors who are paid better than she is despite her having to work harder than they do." I shook my head. "When was the last time she got paid at least equal to her male co-lead?"

"We do not ask that question in my household. That path leads directly to hell and divine punishment. It's been a while."

"By a while, you mean never."

"I really do."

"Imagine if your mother was fairly paid compared to her male co-leads."

"She'd take over the world and have more money than sense."

"She already has more money than sense, Clarissa."

My friend laughed. "Harsh but true. I know you're nervous about the party but try to relax. You'll have a great time, I promise."

Alarms went off in my head; Clarissa didn't make promises unless she meant them, and when she made promises, it meant she had plans to make certain things went her way. "What have you done?"

"Me? I haven't done anything. My mother? My mother has done a lot of interesting things I think are hilarious. Didn't I tell you? She's on a mission to marry us off. She's tired of having single children, and she's adopted you."

"She most certainly has not!"

"She really has. It's too late to run. You're just going to have to deal with my mother's matchmaking ways because there's no way I'm going down alone."

I needed a new life, an escape plan, and a cabin deep in the woods where nobody would ever find me. "I should have known this was a trap."

"You'll survive. I hope. But if a lecher tries anything, shame the fucker."

"Shame the fucker? Don't you mean knee him in the nuts?"

"That could work, but I find humiliation discourages them long term. Pain rarely does more than piss them off."

"How does one shame a lecher?"

"Just tell him his father had better skills in the sack and you should take lessons before trying anything, or ask some hot guy for a kiss to protect you from an unwanted lecher."

"I'm not sexually assaulting a stranger."

"It's not sexual assault if you ask first and he agrees."

Why had I bothered trying to talk sense into a woman wearing an inflatable t-rex costume? I gave up, shook my head, and said, "Fine. If an unwanted lecher tries to get in my face, I'll request permission to sexually assault some hot guy. But will there be any hot single guys present?"

"There'll be plenty. I'm sure you'll have no trouble figuring out who they are. Wedding rings are mandatory, so just check the finger. And if someone is taken but not engaged or married yet, they have to wear a red string. These are strict no-cheating parties, and it's open hunting season on any creep who tries."

"And if the lecher is married?"

"Let me know, and I'll tip off the organizers of all the parties. Cheaters are kicked out."

"That is the coolest party rule I have ever heard. Why is it in place?"

"There are kids present, that's why."

"Good reason. Keep the cheating private, huh?"

"Exactly."

TWO

This is the saddest thing I've ever seen.

TRAFFIC IN MANHATTAN SUCKED, but by some miracle, we reached the condominium complex hosting the party, which towered overhead. The line of limos convinced me I didn't belong at the party, but with so many vehicles clogging the street, I gave up hope of escape.

The crazy woman wearing an inflatable t-rex costume would hunt me down and humiliate me further.

Resigned to my fate, I grabbed the bottle of sparkling wine, popped it open, and split it between the flutes.

There was barely enough in it for half a glass each.

"This is the saddest thing I've ever seen," I announced, holding up the pair of flutes.

"They're props, not fortification for the party. You don't need any alcohol, anyway. It's just a few hours."

"Just a few hours in the shredded ruins of my Prada. My dress will haunt me, I'll be cursed, and entropy will forever follow in my wake."

"I don't think shredding a dress will lead to deterioration wherever you go."

"Chaos, then. I'll be cursed to forever have bad luck."

"It's a dress. It can't curse you."

"You say that now, but you just wait until tomorrow. Mark my words, bad shit will start to happen. I'll go to work and all hell will break loose."

"All hell is going to break loose because you work retail and November is coming, and November sucks. After November is December, and December is your personal hell."

"I need a new job, but I have no applicable life skills, and I'm too damned poor to go to college. The student loans would kill me."

"I can help you figure something out if you want."

"Does it involve handouts?"

"No, it would involve you interviewing for positions that don't require college degrees but do require hard workers willing to learn on the job. I need good people, and degrees aren't everything nowadays. Employers are starting to figure that out. My dad's place is starting to pick people up without the right degrees and train them from scratch because they get better workers for cheaper that way."

"I don't want to be cheaper, Clarissa. I'm tired of being cheaper."

"While cheaper to start with, the banks do tend to promote those who do well, and if you need a degree to qualify, some places are footing the bill without interest because they want good employees. Come on, just trust me for once."

"The last time I trusted you, I shredded my Prada. Now I

have to look out for lechers and might sexually assault a hot guy while trying to escape a lecher."

"The Prada incident is all on you, but the rest is sadly accurate."

"I'm not sure I want to sexually assault a hot guy even with his permission. It's the whole escaping from a lecher part of the equation I'm not a fan of."

"I definitely dislike that part of the equation, too, but sometimes you meet a really nice hot guy in the process. There are a few I wouldn't mind locking lips with here should an opportunity allow."

"Can I settle for asking for one to pretend to be my boyfriend long enough for the lecher to fuck off and die?"

"You forgot about the red string rule."

"I could ask him to ask me to be his girlfriend in front of the lecher. It's for the sake of escape, right? Any decent single man would play along, right?"

The limo pulled up in front of the doors, and Clarissa needed the driver's help to escape the vehicle. I managed even with carrying both champagne flutes, and I handed her glass over so I wouldn't look like a slutty, alcoholic witch. Well, not exactly slutty. For a Prada, it did a rather good job of covering everything of importance.

To make her entrance spectacular, Clarissa pranced towards the doors, holding her flute as high as her t-rex costume would allow. I already regretted everything and, shaking my head, I followed in her wake.

The sparkling wine went down fast, and I longed to smash the empty flute over my friend's head. Without knowing if I held a cheap flute or a fortune in crystal in my hand, I held onto it rather than dumping it into the nearest trash can. Clarissa waged war with the door, pulling when she should have been pushing. To play to her costume choice, she roared.

I took her flute and tossed it back. "If I have to put up with this, I'm drinking your wine."

"Considering I'm working hard to embarrass you, this is fair."

"You're succeeding."

"I know. It's great." Clarissa roared again and plowed through the door, her heels clicking on the marble. She struck a pose. Her next roar came out more like a pterodactyl screech.

I loved my friend, but I really wanted to murder her.

All she needed was for someone to drop a banner from the ceiling.

"I've never been so humiliated in my life." A wretched number of hot men around my age dressed as cowboys, vampires, and as warned, Tarzan, waited for the elevator. The Tarzans had gone the loincloth route, and some of them were so skimpy I made sure to keep my gaze chest high.

"It will get so much worse. So much worse. Just wait until my mother starts introducing you to the Tarzans."

"Speedos have more coverage," I grumbled.

"I'm going to roleplay Godzilla. Follow and watch me work magic."

"Does your magic involve confirming you're insane? If so, you've already cast your spell."

"Rude!"

"Honest."

"Still rude."

"Still honest."

"What do you have against Godzilla?"

"Nothing. Godzilla isn't a t-rex, Godzilla is far cooler

than you ever will be, and you couldn't do Godzilla's roar justice even if you tried." I realized my mistake the instant the words left my mouth. After such a blatant challenge, Clarissa would spend the rest of the night trying to prove she could match Godzilla's roar.

My lunatic friend marched for the crowd waiting for the elevators. "Behold! I am Godzilla, Queen of the Monsters! Make way for my most imperial majesty."

I bowed my head, heaved a sigh, and lifted my hands to rub my temples. "You're a menace."

The crowd laughed, and just as I expected, exactly no one made way for Clarissa, Queen of the Idiots. I'd have to make use of her title at every opportunity. On the other hand, I liked that she enjoyed herself, but she'd pay for making her enjoyment come at my expense.

Revenge would be mine, and when it came, I'd laugh so hard I'd make myself cry.

Clarissa roared again and stomped her heels on the marble. The clicks undermined her pitiful attempts to intimidate the crowd with her vicious dinosaur act. My shoulders shook from the effort of containing my laughter. "You're hopeless, Clarissa."

"No, I'm Godzilla, Queen of the Monsters."

"You're a t-rex suffering from a midlife crisis."

"Rude!"

"Honest."

"This again?"

"Queens aren't supposed to be so sensitive to the commentary of peasants. If you'd like to wait for the elevator, go for it, Little Miss T-Rex, but I'm going to take the stairs, and I don't care how many flights it is. The real dinosaur here is the slow ass elevators." To escape the madness, I headed for the stairwell, which was marked with a helpful sign.

As I refused to carry two flutes up a bazillion steps, and I'd lost my ability to care about the damned glasses, I tossed them into the nearest trashcan. If Clarissa wanted them, she'd have to dig them out, but she could afford to replace them. And if she couldn't, well, she shouldn't have brought them to a Halloween party as part of her costume in the first place.

Maybe if I told myself enough times, I wouldn't feel too guilty over throwing out her property.

To my dismay, several of the vampires, one of the cowboys, and an unfortunate number of the Tarzans thought death by stairwell was a good idea and followed me.

In good news, while tattered, my Prada would preserve my dignity and bar any unwanted men from getting a look at my panties—as would the biker shorts I wore to prevent thigh chafing. They'd have to live with the disappointment. I didn't bother holding the door, as I figured a bunch of testosterone-poisoned males could handle the task on their own.

I estimated I had at least twenty stories to climb, and I refused to accept defeat. I would not surrender, go quietly into the night, or stop until I reached the top floor. Seizing the rail, I climbed.

And climbed. And climbed. And climbed. After four stories, I acknowledged my idiocy rivaled Clarissa's, and that I would have to dub myself Shirley, Empress of the Idiots. Clarissa could be my princess. We'd make a most excellent pair of ruling idiots.

After ten stories, one of the Tarzans did a rather impressive pterodactyl screech. I halted, turned, and admired as a rather fit man my age dramatically fell to his knees on the step while imitating a death scene from Hamlet. He dragged it on for a solid five minutes, and when he finally played dead on the steps, I joined the other stair climbers in giving him a round of applause. "If you're not an actor, you should be. I haven't seen that much drama since the lobby."

My comment earned a laugh from the men, and satisfied I'd taken another step towards claiming my esteemed position as Empress of the Idiots, I resumed my climb.

After what felt like an eternity and made me regret my decision to be stubborn, I reached the top. Some people loitered in the lobby of the penthouse floor, which was manned by several security guards armed with a guest list.

"Has the t-rex suffering from a midlife crisis arrived yet?"

Those gathered laughed and shook their heads. "She's still waiting downstairs. The elevator dinosaurs get tired when overworked, and there's too many people here," yet another Tarzan replied. Of the offerings, he took tall, dark, and handsome to the extreme, his left ring finger was free and clear of ownership markings, and he had some sense of decency, making sure his loincloth covered everything without risk of exposing himself to unsuspecting women. "Which party are you attending?"

"That's a very good question, one the t-rex has the answer to. She begged me to come, and I can't bear to make a full-grown woman cry."

"Your name?"

"Shirley Manchester, but please call me Lee. Clarissa said it was the original party."

"Ah-ha. You'd be with the Garrets, then. If you want to go to the party without Clarissa, turn left, go to the end of the hallway, and turn left again. You can't miss it. I should've known she would've come as a t-rex. She's always up to something. Did she really come as a t-rex? Why is she suffering from a midlife crisis?"

"She's attempting to convince people downstairs she's Godzilla, Queen of the Monsters. She hasn't even had any alcohol, because I took her share. We were supposed to split the glass of sparkling wine, but I needed the fortification after she started screeching like a dinosaur in the lobby."

"I can't say I blame you. I'll be at the third party, so if you want to say hi, ask for me. People know who I am."

Tall, dark, and handsome without a ring needed to come to my party. "You could just come to my party instead. Clarissa will be there, so it's going to be wild. Especially since I think she's dressed up as a hooker vampire under the t-rex costume or something like that. I'm expecting to be followed by lechers, so I need someone my age, single, and easy on the eyes to keep the creeps away, and unlike the other Tarzans in the building, you're not attempting to show off your assets or your ass."

"Clarissa neglected to tell me you were so bold."

"You're not one of her brothers, so you're already a step up. If I wanted a kid in man's clothing, I'd go to the nearest high school."

He laughed. "Wow. That's blunt. I'll note maturity is valued along with some modesty."

"Got a name?"

"David. I have to admit I'm amused I'm being compared to Clarissa's brothers and found to be a step above them. You don't even know me."

"You wear a loincloth well, and you've obviously spent some time at the gym. It's a good look on you. I don't know what you're doing, but keep on doing it."

The elevator opened, and the t-rex suffering from a midlife crisis pranced out. "I have arrived!"

"If I had a knife, a pen, or something, I would pop her," I muttered.

All four security guards offered me their pens. I accepted one with a smile and a nod, and I lifted my impromptu weapon and clicked it. "I will pop you, so help me, Clarissa, I will pop you. I will pop you and drag your deflated ass down the hall if I must."

Clarissa went to her knees and bowed in my direction. "I'm not worthy. I'm not worthy. Don't pop me, please. I'll beg. Don't pop me. I want to wear this again. I want to wear this every day for the rest of my life. I'll do anything, just please don't pop me."

I heaved a sigh and returned the pen to its owner. "I'm so sorry for her."

David offered his arm. "You know what? I think I will skip my party and go to yours instead. You need to be protected from the t-rex suffering from a midlife crisis, and I have to admit, I've never been part of a scheme to protect a woman from lechers before. I feel this will be an educational evening for me. My mother tells me I'm a gentleman in training, and this seems like an excellent opportunity to practice."

I accepted his offer. "Just ignore the t-rex. Maybe if we ignore her for long enough, she'll go away."

"Such a cruel betrayal," Clarissa moaned from the floor.

"You should be grateful I didn't pop you, Clarissa."

"Thank you for not popping me, but please don't abandon me. I loved you first. I loved you more! David's nothing compared to me."

"David has a six-pack and is willing to face off against

lechers. I know everything I need to know. You're dressed like a vampire hooker under that inflatable monstrosity. You're going to attract lechers."

"I really am, but I'm more attractive to lechers than you are. You're not at any risk of popping a boob."

Everyone in the foyer stared at my chest. "I really will pop you, Clarissa."

I lifted my boot to step on her and pop her through some stomping of her person, but David freed his arm from mine, snagged me around the waist, and hauled me away from my soon-to-be-dead friend. "That's my cue to begin a career as a bodyguard. You owe me, Clarissa. You pushed her last button, and even I can see that. My momma didn't raise me to be stupid, and neither did yours."

"You're a traitor, too! Betrayers, betrayers all around me."

"I didn't betray you. I just saved you from being popped. Honestly, you probably deserve it. Actually, you definitely deserve it."

"You are so mean, David." Clarissa crawled after us, and her t-rex head flopped all over the place, forcing her to bat at it, except the costume kept her hands from being able to reach her head.

There was only one thing left for me to do. I pointed and laughed at her while David dragged me away.

I HAD no idea who David was, but everyone loved him, especially the women. It took the single women all of five minutes to make off with him. Clarissa's mother spotted me, clapped her hands, and descended like a hug-hungry vulture.

I braced for her affections and went through the routine, as the woman would cry if she didn't get her hug.

"I was so worried Clarissa would scare you off."

"I wanted to pop her, but David stopped me. I'm not sure why. She's a menace."

The menace had shed her lizard attire, and as warned, strutted her stuff as a hooker vampire. She'd picked a dress designed to showcase her breasts without showing them off, although if she didn't watch herself, she probably would pop a boob and give everyone a show. The skirt covered everything, but I hoped she remembered she couldn't bend over.

"Well, she's dressed better than I expected, honestly. She told me she was going to show up as a stripper halfway through her show. I then reminded her there would be children present, and she changed her plans. Her plan isn't much better, but everything is covered. That's something, right?"

"Your standards have gotten so low, Mrs. Garret."

"With my kids? Sweetheart, I don't have standards anymore. They butchered mine and tossed them out the window. Nowadays, I check in on them to make sure they're still breathing and out of jail. If both of these boxes are checked, it's been a good day."

That explained a lot. "She came dressed up like a wino Godzilla, but she ditched the inflatable costume for the vampire hooker. I feel like I didn't do enough to stop this from happening."

Clarissa's mother checked my dress's tag and clucked her tongue. "Just what I thought. You took scissors to your Prada." Turning away from me, Clarissa's mom drew in a deep breath and hollered, "Juliette? Costume emergency!"

"My costume is not an emergency," I hissed. I pointed at

my belt, which I had slaved away at for hours. "My costume is beautiful."

"Your costume used to be one of Prada's better dresses, and you took scissors to it. Actually, it's gorgeous, and I love what you did with it, but I want to see Juliette's face."

I couldn't tell the age of the woman who approached; she hung somewhere in the middle, neither young nor old, but that precarious place between. She carried herself with pride. "What's wrong? Another popped seam? I have my kit."

"I just wanted you to behold a woman bold enough to cut up a Prada for a witch's costume. Isn't it magnificent? And look at the belt she made. The belt's actually amazing. You might want to start making bejeweled belts like that. I'd buy one without hesitation. You could go with healing crystals, hook in with some shops, and make everyone a killing. This one is great, though. I think she got confused, as she's wearing the belt of a healing witch but dressed up as a dark magic user."

I realized I recognized her from the cover of a fashion magazine, a designer who wore her own clothes, preferred her models to be real people, and catered to the rich and famous. No wonder Clarissa had been so excited.

Juliette Carter made clothes every woman wanted, even me.

I couldn't afford the clothes Juliette Carter made.

Damn.

No wonder my bitch of a friend had been talking about Carter clothes. The woman behind them stood before me, and her mouth hung open, as though she couldn't believe what I'd done to my dress. On that front, I couldn't blame her.

I couldn't believe what I'd done to my dress, either.

"It was all I had," I announced, determined to defend myself against the rich, famous, and out of my league. "I'd saved up for years for this dress, and while it will haunt me into the next life for what I've done to it, it's the only black dress I owned, and I needed a costume for this party."

Juliette Carter dropped to her knees, wrapped her arms around my legs, and cuddled my knees. "Where have you been all of my life? I'm surrounded by people who don't know what a sewing machine is or what it does. You hemmed it. You hemmed it to control the fray. The stitches are orderly and even, so you've used a sewing machine before. You measured. You measured before you cut. You truly measured before you cut. You measured twice before you cut, even."

The entire party came to a halt to behold the sight of a fashion designer clinging to a nobody. "Are you all right, ma'am?"

"Once I'm done worshipping you, I will have my revenge for your horrific treatment of this dress."

I looked to Clarissa's mother for help. "I'm getting some seriously mixed signals from this woman."

"Juliette has a stressful job dealing with clients who do not understand that sewing machines, measuring tape, and other tailoring doohickeys are real things. Juliette's lucky I've seen a sewing machine before, and the rare times I do use mine, I measure four times to make her happy. Unfortunately, I do not have good hand-eye coordination, so I ruin what I attempt to sew anyway, but I do my best."

"Effort counts for something," Juliette mumbled through my dress, still hugging my legs. "I love your stockings, but those shoes need work."

"I'm sorry, Mrs. Carter. I can't afford your shoes or dresses, but they're gorgeous."

"Now you've done it," Clarissa's mother muttered. "No is an allowed answer, Shirley."

"Lee, please. For the sake of my pride, please call me Lee."

"You don't look like a Lee. You're really going to make me call you Lee?"

I pointed at the woman still latched onto my legs. "I'll do this while crying. It's been a long day."

"That's a potent threat, Lee. Please accept the terms of my surrender."

"I didn't ask for surrender, I just asked for you to not call me Shirley."

"It's the same thing, really."

It was? I raised a hand and massaged my temple. "Everyone is staring at us."

"Juliette's half the reason everyone's here. Where she goes, fun happens. I don't think anyone has seen another human being bring Juliette to her knees outside of her close family. She does dramatic death scenes for her husband and son often, and her daughter-in-law got one out of her. Chloe pranced for a week over it, an accomplishment for a very pregnant woman."

"She's not so pregnant now. The baby came early."

In my life, I'd heard entire rooms go still and quiet, but the party went far beyond my expectations. Clarissa's mother frowned. "Is the baby all right?"

"She's fine and dandy, but she'll be staying in the hospital a while until everyone's comfortable. Her name is Candice, and if you would please stay quiet about it, that would be very nice. I've been told I'm banned from hovering until further notice. I want to hover. I need someone to baby. This dress needs to be babied. It was treated so cruelly, weren't you, little one?"

"Its ghost will haunt me, and it will probably murder me for the crimes I've committed against it." Since everyone else took the insanity in stride, I patted Juliette Carter's head. "There, there. It's okay. I'll just dress like a witch every Halloween for the rest of my life to make this travesty at least worth the amount of money I spent on it."

The woman fell to the floor as though I'd stabbed her through the top of her skull. "Chasity, what have you done? What have you wrought upon us? Why? Why have you done this?"

"I didn't. My daughter did. Although honestly, she looks great. Don't cry, Juliette."

"My son is cruelly keeping me from my granddaughter. I should be visiting the baby right now, but no. I'm here." To ensure I couldn't escape, Juliette crawled onto my feet and hugged my ankles. "I have not seen you before, young lady. Please introduce yourself."

"I'm Lee. It's short for Shirley, but I really hate being called Shirley. You've never seen me before because I live in the worst neighborhood Jersey has to offer, whereas you live somewhere around here, I think."

"Hell's Kitchen."

"Do you rule over your kitchen as the incarnation of Satan?"

Someone in the crowd barked a laugh, and a fit of giggling swept through the room.

"It's a neighborhood," Juliette replied with as much dignity as possible for someone sprawled on the floor.

"Well, I suppose you could be the evil ruler of many kitchens in an area deemed to be a neighborhood."

"Damn, Lee. What has gotten into you today, and what do I need to do to invite this you out more often? You're taking Juliette down like she's a shrimp nobody's claimed." Clarissa's mom narrowed her eyes. "And don't you even try to convince me you're not a shameless shrimp addict."

"I dealt with the wino Godzilla and drank her sparkling wine. I needed it to brace for this party. I noticed there was barely enough sparkling wine for a single glass."

My second mother grinned. "I expected one of you would drink whatever was offered, so I prevented any problems by limiting your sparkling wine supply."

"Do you rule as this woman's princess? If so, you should live in Hell's Kitchen instead of in the better parts of Jersey," I muttered.

"Unless you like bored fashion designers dressing you up, I recommend giving Hell's Kitchen a wide berth."

"You are so mean to me, Chasity," Juliette complained.

"You're still mad I wouldn't take you to my last shoot."

"It was in Bali. Any sane woman would be mad they didn't get to go Bali. I would've dressed you to perfection."

"It was for a shoot. You wouldn't have gotten any say in the wardrobe choices."

"I could've changed their mind, but no. I wasn't invited."

Clarissa's mother rolled her eyes. "I'll consider making an appointment for new clothes if you stop tormenting Lee."

"I'm loving her. My love is never a torment. I'll torment her a little later. She does have to pay for modifying one of Prada's perfect dresses. A perfect dress is hard to find, and that dress was perfection. It's not even one of mine, and I have to stand up for the rights of a perfect dress."

"She worked hard to save up for that dress. It is hers to do with as she pleases, even if it means transforming it into a witch's costume. It's a gorgeous costume, Juliette."

"It is, which is why I'm torn between immediately seeking revenge on behalf of that dress and loving her. Right now, I'm loving her. I have an urge to replace her shoes, though. These are not a good shoe. I may have to target these shoes as part of my revenge."

Why had I gone with Clarissa's idea to go to the party? Right. She was my friend. "And to think I was worried about lechers. I didn't realize fashion designers were a Halloween party hazard."

"Oh, you'll get those later, I'm sure. They wait to come out until after the kids have left. If you want to avoid the old lechers, you leave when the families with kids leave. Until then, most behave," my designer attachment replied. "I'll consider putting a stay on revenge if you let me deal with your shoe problem."

"No."

"Wow, Chasity. She's ruthless."

"She works in retail, and the holiday season is approaching. She works at a boutique in Jersey."

"I haven't done the Jersey circuit before. It's so…Jersey."

"That's why you've never seen her. Had you gotten over yourself and your dislike for my state, you would've met her already. But she would have been working the floor at the time, and she'd hate you right now for the chaos you bring to any boutique unfortunate enough to have to deal with you."

Wow. Clarissa's mother rarely went for another woman's throat, but when she did, she unsheathed her verbal claws, sharpened them, and meant business.

"Just because you speak the truth does not mean you should say the truth. What did I ever do to you?"

"I saw Lee first. She's mine, and you can't have her."

Wow, wow, wow. I caught sight of Clarissa, shot her a glare, and pointed at the fashion designer on my feet.

My friend flipped me the bird and stuck her tongue out.

I worried I wouldn't escape the party with my sanity intact. In what world were lechers safer than fashion designers?

Mine.

Damn. I needed a new life before my current one got tired of my shit and finished me off.

THREE

I'd never thought my crystal belt and Prada witch's dress would be the most normal outfit.

CLARISSA'S MOTHER saved me from a fate worse than death. The instant Juliette Carter released my ankles, I fled. To keep the fashion designer from latching onto me, I did the only sane thing I could do under the circumstances: I abandoned the first party and tested my luck in the hallway. Other partygoers had opted for the hallway party, too, transforming the place into a maze of people dressed in absurd outfits.

I'd never thought my crystal belt and Prada witch's dress would be the most normal outfit. Vampires were common, as were werewolves. The Tarzan trend annoyed me, and I came to the conclusion that the men dressed as Tarzan were single lechers hoping to have their loincloths removed.

Ugh.

How the hell was I supposed to find a decent man not at high risk of being a lecher? David had seemed decent enough, but he classified as one of the men looking for some late-evening action. He'd taken the dive into the fray of single ladies and enjoyed their attention. Players went onto my 'hell no' list, and he showed most symptoms of a chronic player.

Maybe I could slip out of the party, get a cab, and head home. I'd miss the money later, but I expected the public transit system would be the end of me if I attempted to make my way home on my own.

"Hey, babe. Nice dress, but you'd look better out of it," one of the many Tarzans said, sidling up to me.

As I had no interest in being subjected to his offerings, I didn't even turn my head in his direction. "No, thanks."

"Come on, baby. I'm the best you'll ever have."

What was it with rich men and their egos? Why couldn't they buy a personality and dignity with their money? Damn it, I'd been at the party for less than an hour, and I already needed a gentleman willing to deal with me and play dumb while I used him as an escape route.

Even David would do, as a player beat a man who didn't understand the meaning of the word no.

"Not interested."

"You'll like it."

I wanted to ram my knee into his groin and give a good twist while I was at it, but his money would make my assault of his delicate, fragile self stick, and I didn't want to spend half my life in jail for giving an asshole a reason to leave me alone. The hallway party had plenty of men, and few wore rings or strings.

If I eliminated all the Tarzans, I had some vampires, a werewolf, and someone around my age dressed in a suit. I had no idea if the suit was a costume or not, but I'd take him home to meet Mom on appearances alone. A quick check of his left finger revealed he wasn't claimed.

My ploy probably wouldn't work, but I marched over in his direction.

"Hey! I wasn't done talking to you."

Damned egotistical bastard. In good news, his outcry caught attention, including the brown-haired man I'd chosen as my escape route. The vampire accompanying him raised a brow, and I recognized one of Clarissa's brothers.

I really needed a new life. My current one really hated me and wished for me to die. Sighing, I beelined for Jonas. "Is your friend the kind your mother would let Clarissa date?"

"Unfortunately for my peace of mind, yes," Clarissa's brother replied. "You have an attachment."

"Unwanted." I stared Jonas's friend in the eye. "Please help get rid of him. I'm paying in a kiss, but that's all you're getting out of me unless it's a friendly coffee date."

He chuckled. "I can't say I've ever been part of such a rescue mission before, but I'm happy to oblige. I'll skip the cheesy pickup lines since you've offered the invitation, if you please."

Damn. I'd found a man who came prepackaged with the word please. "I do please, actually. Thank you."

I'd played the kissing game enough times to hold my ground, and my partner of choice wasted no time going in for the kill. His arm wrapped around my waist and pulled me close while his lips went after my self-respect first and scored a knock-out. Unsatisfied with that, he went for gold and hit it right out of the park. If we'd been at a baseball game, the ball would've been long gone, likely out on the street beyond the stands and the parking lot.

Hot damn. He needed a warning label to prevent unsuspecting women like me from playing with fire. He stopped before he crossed the line to indecent, pulled away, and smirked. His attention settled on my unwanted attachment. "The next time a lady tells you no, it doesn't mean ask until she says otherwise."

While keeping one arm wrapped around me, he pointed down the hall. "I just thought you'd like to know your boss is over there and saw the whole thing."

Tarzan turned a rather unpleasant shade of green, and he spun around and fled.

"Well, that was a most unexpected but enjoyable twist to my evening. Jonas, I trust you'll keep the lady company? If I don't leave now, I'll miss my meeting. Mind serving as the go-between on our coffee date since you two know each other?"

"Sure thing. Drive safely. It's a madhouse out there."

I admired the view when he left. "Do I want to know who he is, Jonas?"

"He owns the penthouse hosting the third party. Does that answer your question?"

"It really does. Now I'm really glad I asked before just randomly kissing him. That was my other option. I was starting to get desperate. I figured he couldn't be too bad if he were hanging out with you."

"That's a really low bar. I just thought you should know that."

"Better than that lowlife Tarzan incapable of understanding English."

"As my mother will literally murder me if someone does anything to you tonight, care to have a tour of the third party? If my esteemed opinion doesn't ensure that you don't want to know who he is, his penthouse will."

"It beats just standing in the hallway waiting for another lecher to try his luck."

"Why are you in the hallway, anyway? Mom was determined to ghost you all night long."

"She's fighting with a fashion designer last I checked. I have angered the fashion designer, and she claims she will be seeking revenge. I'm concerned, as she now knows which state I live in."

"Juliette?"

I laughed. "How did you guess?"

"There's only one designer here who would openly seek revenge against someone, and it's her. What did you do?"

I gestured to my dress. "It used to be a Prada. Now it's a witch's costume. Apparently, it's a perfect Prada."

"I'm not sure I can protect you from Juliette, but I'll try. Mom will be proud of me for a change. I'll play your date, but you're not getting a red string out of me. I value my life." Jonas held out his arm. "Plus, I get to tell my sister my costume was being your date rather than a vampire."

I linked my arm with his. "Sounds like a plan. I like you, but you're not dating material, Jonas."

"You may not be from money, but you make our standards look low. And that's not a bad thing. That's why Mom likes you so much. You haven't gotten anywhere, but you haven't settled, and she loves you for it. She also loves Other Mom's cooking."

"Yeah. I couldn't date you even if I liked you. You're too much like a brother at this point, and that's gross."

"On that, we're agreed. Also, thank you for not being born a man, Lee. It would be awkward."

"Why?"

"I'm that gay friend you never knew was gay, and I'd have to fight my sister over you. As I said, awkward."

Damn. "Cool. Do you do hair?"

"As a matter of fact, yes."

"I need a cut and I'm too cheap to go to a salon. What does a girl have to do to get you to fix this disaster?"

"I'll swing by tomorrow. I have the day off work. That work for you?"

"You can dye it whatever color you want, too. You could even perm it. I don't care, just make me look pretty for a change. The boutique has decided to 'welcome all hairstyles and colors to allow our store to be more in line with modern trends.' Actually, I just want a really good disguise, so the fashion designer doesn't find me. Don't remind that guy about the coffee date, by the way. He's probably one of New York's Most Eligible Bachelors, and I just can't handle that level of responsibility."

Jonas led me down the hall, turned the corner, and kept walking until we reached the end. "So, about this building. There are four penthouses. His is the largest of them and has the best view. While he opened his penthouse for the party, he has a security detail on hand. It's very much look and don't touch. I'm on the list to have full access to the penthouse, so if you want to escape the mayhem, we can go into his private entertainment room and play some console games. Also, there are two levels, and you probably don't want to know how much it cost."

"Trust fund?"

"Inheritance from a relative, good business sense, and the inability to keep from working," Jonas replied. "For a workaholic, he's a good person. He doesn't have time for a girlfriend or a wife. He might even ask about that date. It's been a while since he's had an excuse to go out with someone as friends, and that is how you framed it. Honestly, he probably played along because you set the stage as a friendship with a kiss rather than wanting in his pants."

I definitely wanted in his pants, but as I didn't jump into bed with random men without a damned good reason or an engagement ring, I'd have to daydream about him in his perfect suit. I'd learned my lesson after a few bad men, and nobody was getting an easy ticket for a night of fun out of me anymore. "Hey, that's pretty impressive. I didn't completely screw it up."

"It's okay. I would've rescued you even if he hadn't gone with it. That guy you dodged is an asshole."

"More of an asshole than you are?"

Jonas laughed. "Sweetheart, while I'm at least a princely asshole, he's a crowned ruler of assholes. He's got six kids because he doesn't like when a woman tells him he has to wear a condom. I would've hated to have had to introduce him to my knuckles for trying to pull that shit on you."

"Damn. That's awful."

"So is his child support bill. You'd figure he'd learn, but no. Turns out the bastard's a shitty asshole, but he's a great dad. The only thing he loves more than screwing women are his kids. If it weren't for that, I would've hit him for even looking at you."

I would never understand people. "Please tell me his kids aren't here."

"Nah. As I said, he's a shitty human being unless his kids are involved, then he's the perfect example for all dads to follow. I don't get it, and I doubt I ever will, but that's all right. Oh, Lee?"

"What?"

"Do me a favor."

"What do you need?"

"When we go into my friend's penthouse, please don't scream."

What had I gotten myself into?

WOMEN SCREAMED FOR MANY REASONS. Some screamed when they saw the perfect pair of shoes. Others screamed if a spider crossed their path. I screamed if winged assassins with butt knives tried to sting me.

Hospital visits sucked, as did slowly suffocating to death. I appreciated the slowly part of the equation; I didn't need to carry an allergy pen with me as long as I sought out medical attention within an hour. At that point, my body gave up hope. Popping allergy pills helped, but ultimately, I needed to cart my ass to the nearest doctor if I wanted to stay reasonably safe.

Not even Clarissa knew the real reason behind my screams when a winged assassin with a butt knife crossed my path.

I hoped to keep it that way.

A Leonardo da Vinci drawing decorated the entry, and a pair of security guards kept the curious from getting too close to it. It rendered me speechless, and had it been unguarded, I would've spent hours lovingly stroking its frame.

Everyone in Clarissa's family knew my dirty little secret, my crush on old sketches that embraced the unfinished beauty of life.

In many ways, I viewed myself as a sketch, an unfinished piece lacking color. I wanted to be beautiful, too, like the profile sketch of a woman's face, the hint of a smile on her lips.

Her eyes kept secrets, and I could lose hours attempting to decipher them.

There was only one thing I could say. "Can the coffee date involve sitting on the floor underneath that picture and staring at it for hours?"

"I'm going to do you a favor and not tell him you have a crush on his sketch."

"How is that doing me a favor?"

"It's his prized possession."

Damn it. I'd found the perfect rich man, and he didn't have time for a woman. Still, I could dream. "Then a coffee date sitting beneath it would be perfect. Just look at it, Jonas. It's a masterpiece."

"It's a barely finished drawing."

"That's what makes it a masterpiece." I huffed at Jonas's lack of refined taste in art. "You will be pleased to learn I wouldn't scream over just seeing a painting. I wouldn't even scream if he offered to let me take it home."

"You wouldn't? What would you do?"

"Cry or faint," I admitted. "That sketch is worth more than I am."

"I disagree."

"I don't. I understand that sketch's worth."

Jonas rolled his eyes and pointed at one of two hallways branching off the foyer. "You're worth more than some dumb sketch."

Somehow, revealing his interest in other men had done Jonas a world of good. Any other day, he would've just laughed at me. "You being nice is seriously starting to creep me out, I just thought you should know this."

"Being a prince of assholes is hard work, so I'm on vacation right now. You're going to have to deal with the kind and considerate version, although I will deny any and all accusations should you attempt to tell anyone I can be a kind and considerate being."

If Jonas brought out his kind and considerate version, I could understand why the penthouse's owner stayed friends with him. The penthouse belonged to someone with good taste and more money than possibly god. While I didn't recognize many of the painters, his walls showcased fine art, the kind bought for millions at auction. I wanted to spend the rest of my life, or a minimum of several weeks, examining each painting. "He collects art."

"It is his vice and passion. He'd rather work ten or more hours a day to come home and spend the rest of his day staring at paintings on the wall than having a life. Since he doesn't have a woman to waste his money on, he can spend it on anything he likes."

I saw no problems with the man's life choices. I'd be forever curious about how he'd learned to be such a damned fine kisser, though. Then again, if he didn't have time for women, maybe he took lessons from the local street ladies. That would put a damper on my day, as the last thing I needed was a bill to be tested for anything I might've picked up from kissing a promiscuous male. I'd hope for natural talent. Natural talent wouldn't create any long-term trouble for me. "And?"

"And what?"

Pointing at the nearest painting, depicting flowers in a vase, I glared at Clarissa's brother.

"They're daisies, I think. And?"

"Life doesn't have to be about going out after work and

dealing with assholes. The art seems healthier, anyway. There are a lot of assholes in the world."

"While I'm not disputing the population of the kingdom I'm in line to rule, I don't feel that you understand the severity of his introverted behavior."

"Jonas."

"What?"

"I'm an introvert. Your sister is an extrovert. Do you know what extroverts do to introverts?"

"I'm afraid to ask, but I'm going to ask anyway. What do extroverts do to introverts?"

"Adopt them and force them to leave their homes."

Jonas snorted. "He doesn't make a good introvert except when he's not working, which is not often."

"Well, after working so hard, I wouldn't want to deal with people, either."

"I feel this is an important time to remind you that you work in retail, Lee."

I sighed. "I never claimed I made good life choices. It just happens to be the one job I'm good at. I can't afford college, not that it would do me any good. I'm good at selling clothes. I'm bad at going to school. I'm useless at school, really. Lectures make me want to stab people, I don't write notes fast enough, and I can't remember what was said after five minutes if I don't write it down. Now, if they could just give me a damned book and ask me to read it, I would be okay. But for some reason, colleges expect to lecture students. You should be proud of me for refusing to waste money on an education I'd flunk out of due to an inability to handle lectures."

"It can't possibly be that bad."

"It can possibly be that bad. I didn't go to college because my grades in high school are a horror show. I wouldn't earn financial aid, as I couldn't keep my damned head any higher than C level."

"At least a C counts as a passing grade."

"Barely." I bowed my head. "They don't care about your grades in retail. They care about your ability to kiss ass. Does the person in the store make good money and want to buy clothes? Kiss ass. Don't tell the lady looking at the black slinky cocktail dress she'll look like an undead raven. That is how you get fired from retail."

"I'm going to guess one of your co-workers did that?"

"Yes, she did. You're a professional liar in retail, Jonas. You tell the customer what they want to hear and hope for the best. If you get a unicorn, they should be worshipped."

"Dare I ask what a unicorn is?"

"It's the man or woman who has no idea what to buy, they understand they have no idea what they're doing, and they ask for help. Not only do they ask for help, they listen to the advice offered. They tell you their budget, they let you dress them up so they look nice, and they buy what you suggest. They leave the store with good clothes for them, and everyone is happy with the transaction. That is the unicorn. I love unicorns."

"When was the last time you got a unicorn?"

I slumped my shoulders and pouted. "It's been a while. I usually get the demons."

"Why do you get the demons?"

"My boss hates me and wishes for me to relocate my skinny ass to hell."

"Does your boss actually hate you?"

"She keeps referring the demons to me. I am assigned clients, Jonas. Some of these demons call my manager, demand to know my schedule, and expect me to be there to cater to their every whim."

"Well, you do work in a high-end boutique. Some of those dresses cost thousands, right?"

"It's where I bought my Prada. For the record, there is no employee discount on dresses like this Prada."

"That's just harsh."

"So was its price tag."

"I think we need to go to the entertainment room and kill zombies for the duration of this party. I'm not sure I want to see what happens if one of the demons you cater to happens to be at one of the parties. Also, I question why they call it going postal because your tone of voice implies you're ready to go retail on some demon's ass."

"Was it that obvious?"

"The scorn in your voice over your lack of an employee discount on your dress sent the message loud and clear. Also, as part of my catering services as your gay friend, not only am I going to cut your hair, we are going shopping."

"With what money?"

"Mine. Possibly my mother's. If I'm in a mood, I'll steal some of dad's money. It'll be an early Christmas present, and I refuse to take no for an answer. Also, we never discuss this happened. I will dress you up, and then my sister and the rest of my family can question where you got your spectacular new wardrobe."

I worried for Jonas. "Are you mentally impaired or drunk?"

"No, I just recognize I've been that demonic asshole, and I wish to make it up to the only retail person I know personally."

Pride came before the fall, but who needed pride when I

had my very own gay friend to take me shopping? "Will you make me pretty?"

"You're already pretty, but I'll make you beautiful instead. How does that sound?"

"Like you're crazy, but let's go murder some zombies. I feel a need to destroy something. In a game will do."

"I've never been more grateful zombies aren't real, as your tone of voice implied you'd take the fight to real-life given a baseball bat and an opportunity."

"It's been a long life."

"So it has. Let's go teach those zombies a lesson."

FOUR

Does the favor involve murder?

I COULDN'T HIT the broad side of a barn in the game we played, but I loved smashing zombies in the face with anything I could get my hands on. Jonas preferred to do his zombie hunting from a distance. While he slaughtered me on the survivability front, I'd beaten him in body count, leaving a trail of mutilated undead corpses in my wake.

"Do me a favor, Lee."

I grunted as I'd spied my next victim, some businessman whose suit needed some major work. I tapped the button to sift through my weapon choices and, after a moment of thought, picked the machete. I hadn't done nearly enough zombie killing with a machete, and the suit needed to be put out of its misery along with the undead. I hammered the buttons, huffing when I secured my brutal victory over yet another member of the scourge attempting to end the world. "Does the favor involve murder?"

"Not exactly."

I went on a hunt for my next target. "I'm not sure I'm interested if the favor doesn't involve murder."

"Could you save a few for me?"

"If you'd stop trying to sneak up on a damned zombie so you can sniper them, you'd have more zombies to kill. I'm pretty sure I watched you walk by at least three crowbars. The crowbars are really satisfying, especially if it gets stuck in their face."

"I've never been so scared of a woman in my life."

"I'm not the reason you're gay, Jonas."

"The reason I'm gay doesn't involve terror of women, this is true. Men are more appealing."

"I never thought I'd say I agree with you on something like this, but yes, men are more appealing to me than women."

"I'm open to browsing photos of tastefully nude men and discussing their assets."

"His assets or his ass?"

"Can the answer be both?"

I didn't have to think about that one for long. "Only if we can objectify men in kilts. I have a thing for men in kilts, Jonas."

"Only if the kilts are being worn properly."

I would never understand why people didn't like gay men. Gay men made the best conversationalists. "For that, I am saving you a few zombies, but if one comes up behind me and eats my brains again, we will have words."

"You'll have words. They're curses. I'll just laugh."

"There's the asshole I know and love. Is it really all right for us to hide down here and play video games?"

"He won't mind."

"Does he have a name, or am I just going to have to think of him as the penthouse guy?"

Jonas took his time thinking about that. "He likes his privacy, and he's had issues with women in the past."

I understood; society had women trained to want the rich men who were ahead in life, no matter how poorly they behaved. Wealth and power meant more than happiness. I'd met enough rich, unhappy people to clue in money didn't bring happiness, although stuff could make one happy for a little while. "Penthouse Guy it is. I don't need to know his name, although now I'm feeling particularly awkward I'd locked lips with the Penthouse Guy without bothering to learn his name."

"Yeah. That did surprise me, although considering who was hassling you, I would've kissed some strange dude, too."

"And you being gay has nothing to do with that?"

"Despite general appearances, I do have standards."

"Like asking him his name first?"

Jonas sighed. "Yep."

"Does this get me labeled as a slut or a whore? I was never sure where the distinction was."

"Whores are paid, sluts aren't. You didn't take it far enough to earn either label, I'm afraid. You were only slightly naughty."

"Considering I'm generally a stick in the mud, I accept my new designation as a slightly naughty woman without complaint."

"I thought you were a stick in the mud because you got tired of men thinking with only their dicks?"

"That, too."

"The Penthouse Guy is capable of rational thought that doesn't involve his sexual parts."

Huh. Miracles could happen. "I question how he's still single. Do you know how hard it is to find a half-decent man capable of thinking with his brain rather than his trouser trout?"

"Did you just call penises trouser trout?"

"Yes." I hunted for another zombie and found a hillbilly with a broken beer bottle in his hand.

Hmm. I wondered if the game counted a broken beer bottle as a weapon. Determined to find out, I selected my baseball bat and went hunting for my next toy. The hillbilly went down without getting a chance to swing at me.

"I thought you were going to save me some."

"He had a broken beer bottle." I checked the body, delighted to discover the bottle did count as a usable weapon. "It's now my broken beer bottle, and I'm about to go shank a zombie with it."

"I think I need to take you shopping for an upgraded television and a game console for Christmas. I had no idea you liked these games so much."

"Me, myself, and I had no idea killing zombies could be so damned enjoyable, Jonas." It'd be too much to ask to just visit the Penthouse Guy and his paintings and play on his system. "Is a television and console and some of these games more expensive than my poor Prada?"

"Substantially cheaper."

I thought about it. "And it's not mooching if it's a Christmas present?"

"It's not mooching if it's a Christmas present, I promise. It's not mooching at all, because you deserve nice things, too."

Since when? I'd have to put some thought into that later. "Let me kill a zombie with my beer bottle, then you can convince me if I need one of these with some other games. Don't disappoint me, Jonas."

My best friend's brother laughed. "How would you like to crash some cars we can never afford? You get bonus points for stylish crashes."

What had I been missing all of my life? "I want to drive the most expensive car in the game, and I want to go out in a blaze of glory."

"You got it, babe." Jonas set his controller aside. "Get your beer bottle rampage out of your system, and I'll introduce you to the real wonders of the console world."

"SERIOUSLY, JONAS?"

I ignored the voice of the man I'd used to escape a creeper, all of my attention focused on crushing my best friend's brother in our race. The bastard hated to lose and went out of his way to make me crash, and for the first time in the entire night, his headlights graced my rearview mirror.

Jonas yelped, and while he crashed his car, I sped towards victory, hammering at the booster button to make my sporty beast of a vehicle go a little faster. When I crossed the finish line, I squealed and waved my controller in victory. "Suck that, Jonas!"

"That's not fair!"

"I refuse to surrender my victory. Refuse. I would've beaten you anyway."

For once.

"He distracted me."

"That's not my fault, is it?" I set the controller down,

groaned, and flopped on the couch. "I'm so tired."

"There's a reason for that," Manhattan's best kisser replied. "It's four in the morning."

Huh. I digested that news, wondered if I cared, and considered my work situation. Somehow, I'd have to hike back to Jersey, make it to the boutique for a half-day of work, and find some time to sleep around that. "Damn. My shift starts at nine. Well, I'm screwed."

Or not. Groaning, I grabbed the nearest cushion and covered my head with it. "It's Jonas's fault. He promised to show me the world of console games, and my beer bottle rampage took forever."

"You were killing zombies with broken beer bottles, weren't you?"

"The crowbar is pretty fun, too."

"I see. Did you have a good time?"

"Please never tell anyone I had a good time; I will never live it down."

Jonas snickered. "She begged me for just one more race every time I beat her. I had all my turbos left, and if it hadn't been for you, I would've beaten her again."

Bastard. "You're evil."

"I'm just better at car racing games than you are. I even humored you and changed games how many times?"

"I lost count."

"He has a few more car racing games."

Jonas's stupidly rich friend sighed. "When I said you could play video games if the assholes came out in force, I didn't mean until four in the morning, Jonas."

"Well, you should have specified that, then. Look, I even brought a nice girl home."

"You're gay. You don't want to bring a nice girl home.

And you visit my home because I'm not gay but don't give a shit who you're dating. If you meant to bring a nice girl home for me, that requires me to be home when you do so."

I might consider ditching my ring policy for a night or six for the Penthouse Guy. He'd maintain his rank as Manhattan's best kisser by default, as I had no intention of kissing anyone else or attend any parties where I might need to pull another dumbass stunt involving kissing a stranger.

"While that's true, have mercy. I almost got it right that time."

Jonas's friend grunted. "You're not supposed to get it right, idiot. You're gay. Get out of my house."

"I would, but I'm so very tired, and someone has to take Lee back to Jersey."

I groaned at the thought of trying to make it back to Jersey at four in the morning. "This is going to suck so bad. This is all your fault, Jonas."

"Actually, it's my sister's fault. She made you come to the party in the first place. Then she showed up wearing an inflatable dinosaur costume. That's pretty traumatizing."

Yes, it was. "It's still your fault, and I have no idea how the hell I'm getting home."

"In good news for you, I have business in Delaware today, so detouring to Jersey won't inconvenience me much. I will hold this over Jonas's head for the rest of his life, however."

Damn. The nameless bachelor not only participated in random rescue missions against creeps, but he also seemed to be genuinely nice, too. Well, shit. "I was thinking I'd hold out my hand to my best friend's idiot brother and make him pay me the ridiculous amount required to cab home so I can get ready for work."

"In that case, I'll call a driver for you, and I'll send Jonas the bill. I'll also add interest and a requirement for general enslavement."

"You should make him style my hair extra pretty tonight." I peeked out from under the cushion. "Extra pretty, Jonas."

"If you forgo the color, I'll curl it. What time do you get off?"

"I was supposed to be off today, but someone needed to come in three hours late, so I'm covering her shift. I'll be done no later than one." I should've been done no later than noon, but I doubted I'd make it out before one, not with the holiday hell season swiftly approaching. Then again, I counted myself lucky; I'd only gotten over thirty hours the past few weeks because of people needing to miss a few hours of their shift. If I got lucky, I'd go over forty hours, which would make my life a little easier. "I should've mentioned that before I asked if you were available tomorrow."

"It just means I get to sleep in."

"Then it's settled," Jonas's friend announced. "Here. Put your address into the app, so the driver knows where to take you."

I emerged from beneath the cushion, took his phone, the kind of device I drooled over but could never own, and tapped in my address before handing it back to him. He touched the screen and nodded. "Fifteen minutes. Jonas, why don't you escort her to the lobby? I'll tell security you're supposed to be here."

"They know I'm supposed to be here. They would've kicked me out otherwise."

"I knew I shouldn't have told them to ignore you and your guest. A mistake on my part."

Without any sign of offense or shame, Jonas hopped to

his feet and planted a kiss on his friend's cheek. "You know you love me."

Damn. Not only was Jonas's friend hot, considerate, and generally friendly, he showed zero evidence Jonas's behavior bothered him. "I love tormenting you."

I kissed my heart goodbye, wished it well on its journey, and wondered if copious amounts of alcohol I couldn't afford might erase my memories of the perfect man. As I doubted a bender would help, I scratched it off my to-do list and decided chocolate would do the trick instead. "I would say I'm sorry for him, but if I had to apologize for every dumbass stunt Jonas pulled, we'd be here for a few years."

"Isn't that the honest truth? If you're so inclined, Jonas rather abhors museums and classical art. You could request he style your hair to match a painting."

"No." Jonas crossed his arms and glowered. "Absolutely not."

"I recommend ringlets with a tiara, and if you were particularly keen on making him pay for his various misdeeds, he knows where to acquire period gowns."

I stared at Jonas. "Why do you know where to acquire period gowns?"

"I have an actress for a mother and an insane sister who likes dressing up as weird things."

Poor Jonas. "Okay. I'm sorry. You're right. I should have immediately realized that. I now feel guilty I haven't rescued you from the insanity that is your life. Will you forgive me?"

"I'll think about it. If you don't make me buy you a period gown."

"But I want to be as pretty as one of the ladies in a painting."

If looks could kill, Jonas would've had me in my grave in ten seconds flat. "You're a terrible human being."

"But I want to be pretty. Make me pretty, Jonas."

"Fine. Revenge will be coming, and when it does, you only have yourself to blame."

I shrugged. "I already stirred the ire of a fashion designer tonight. Do your worst. It can't be as bad as what that woman will do to me should she find out where I live or work."

"Pardon?" Jonas's friend asked.

"She cut up one of Prada's perfect dresses, and Juliette Carter found out about it. I've been getting texts all night about it. Juliette performed a few death scenes from Hamlet over it. Lee's now the talk of all three parties."

I was? "You had time to check your phone?"

"You went to the bathroom three times tonight. I also peeked when you were trying to find a game you might beat me at."

Huh. "Now I'm really glad I didn't stay for the actual parties. One close encounter of the creep kind is enough for me for one day. I would've hated if everyone wanted to have a talk with me before Juliette Carter gets her hands on me and finishes me off."

Jonas's friend snickered. "Or worse, dresses you up."

I'd seen most of Carter's clothes, and I would've given an arm and a leg to own a single piece. "I had no idea that could possibly count as a punishment."

"Just trust me on this one. That woman has little self-restraint and is on a mission to bring out the best in people."

I couldn't see the problem with someone wanting to bring out the best in people in a world like the one we lived in. "I value my life and don't wish to die at the hands of a fashion designer. But Jonas will save me. He'll transform me into an entirely different person tomorrow after work. I just have to last until then, right?"

"I wish you the best of luck with that. Jonas, do let me know how that works out for her. I think I'll plan our coffee meeting to celebrate her survival. Keep me in the loop." Jonas's friend checked his phone. "The driver will be here soon."

I took that as my cue to get the hell out of his penthouse. I grabbed my purse, checked to make sure I had everything, and dragged Jonas out by his ear before I said something else I'd regret.

THE NEXT TIME someone stupidly rich offered to get me a driver, I needed to remember they were too posh and egotistical to hire cabbies. A limo pulled up within moments of stepping outside of the condominium building. I stared at the sleek, black vehicle, and I heaved a sigh. "He got a limo, Jonas."

"Please tell me you weren't expecting one of those random driver services."

"I totally was. That's normal. And a lot cheaper."

"Well, I'm paying the bill, as I should. I did block you from catching your ride home."

"I wouldn't say you blocked me. You lured me into playing ridiculous games all night long. Also, I really am going to budget to get one of those for myself."

"I already told you I'd buy it and the television needed. But in exchange, you must play with me at least once a month."

"While I'm not a good opportunist, even I can recognize a deal when it crosses my path. I want all of the car racing games and that zombie game."

"I'll toss in a few good single-player games for you, too. You still into those puzzle games?"

"Always." I usually played on my piece of shit laptop, which really needed to be tossed into a dumpster and lit on fire. "Do you accept payment plans?"

"You know what? I'm just going to go home with you and crash on your couch tonight. That way, we can talk about this scheme of yours. You have captured my attention."

I lived paycheck to paycheck, but with a little time and a lot of effort, I'd make a better situation for myself—and I'd be brave enough to ask for help. I would also ask for help without wallowing in guilt for doing it.

Change began with me, and while I'd never live in a fancy penthouse with beautiful paintings, I could improve my situation.

"My couch is always available for your use, but I make no promises you'll like it."

"If I don't, I'll buy you a new couch, as I'm a spoiled rotten brat and can't sleep on busted springs."

I wouldn't tell Jonas about the busted springs—or where I'd initially gotten the couch in the first place. There were limits to how far I could push the rich boy. I had gone through the effort of detoxing it several times before using it, though.

He'd survive. Probably.

The limo driver got out and held open the door for me. Resigned to my unexpected sleepover party, I thanked him and climbed in, and Jonas joined me, taking the seat across from me. "This is insane, I hope you know. Some crazy stalker person is going to see us leave together and think we're dating. Worse, they're going to think we're sleeping together."

"Almost everyone attending all three parties knows I'm hiding out in the closet. Those who haven't heard it from me have probably figured it out."

"I guess you're telling me I'm dense and blind."

"No, you just don't give a shit about my sexual orientation. You're also my sister's friend."

"Your sister is a pain in my ass."

"While this is true, you still like her."

"She's a crazy but fun pain in my ass, and she has an unexpectedly high tolerance for destitution."

"I'm now concerned about what I'm going to find in your apartment."

"You should have thought of that before inviting yourself over for the night."

"I should have. You're right. I will quietly accept my punishment for my oversights. So, what is this payment plan you want?"

"I have a cheap laptop that can't actually do anything but use a browser and online apps, and it doesn't even do a good job at that. I thought it might be time to get something a little better."

"What's your budget?"

"That's the bad news."

"Just hit me with it."

"If I don't waste money on things like costume parties, I usually have twenty or thirty dollars left over when I'm paid. But that's only after a good week where I picked up extra hours."

Jonas winced. "Okay. That explains a few things. Mom

had sent me a text asking if you were all right because, for a minute there, you looked like Juliette had ripped your heart out of your chest and stepped on it."

"I saved for two years to get this dress, and I made my budget as tight as possible to be able to afford it. And I cut it up for a costume party, and now a fashion designer is after my soul. I didn't want to humiliate Clarissa, but then she showed up in an inflatable dinosaur costume."

"Which you probably couldn't have afforded without warning anyway."

"But I could've shown up as a peddler or something. I could've grabbed my pennywhistle and played sad music in the hallway to collect change."

"You do not have a pennywhistle, and you would not do such a thing."

"Go ahead, Jonas. Try me."

"Please, no. I will do anything you want, just don't go out on a street corner with a pennywhistle playing for tips."

I snorted. "Would a harmonica be a better choice?"

"No."

"Ukulele?"

"Definitely not."

"Hurdy-gurdy?"

"Also, a no."

"How about a kazoo?"

"What is wrong with you?"

"Nothing! I'm just saying it's worth considering." I had mad pennywhistle skills, too. With boredom a constant enemy, I battled it the few ways I could, and trolling pawn-shops for cheap instruments I could toy with helped battle my awareness of my inability to make any headway in life. "How about a harp?"

The mid-sized harp had been my crowning achievement of pawnshop trolling, and my parents had gotten it restored for me as a Christmas present a few years ago. I'd never be able to afford a piano, but the harp worked wonders for my mood.

"I'll tell you what, Lee. You show up at a park with a harp and earn even a dollar playing, and I'll buy you a good laptop for Christmas. When my family asks what is wrong with me, I will tell them I sold my soul to the devil tonight."

I played my best when tired as hell and relying on my fingers to do all the remembering for me, so I had some hope of suckering some kind soul for a dollar. "While I am at work, I expect you to pick up a period gown that should fit me. Then you will make me as pretty as one of the Penthouse Guy's paintings, and we will go to a park, and I will play my harp for you, and should I get even a single dollar, you will buy me that computer afterward."

"Deal. Just don't cry when you get booed off nature's stage. I am also picking the park, and I will tell my friends about our bet, and they will not give you a tip unless you are a suitably talented performer. I'm going to tell my artsy friends. But if you're lucky, a few of the ladies might get dressed up, so you don't feel like a complete idiot. They're nice people like that."

Jonas would pay for his lack of faith, and I'd enjoy it. "Deal."

FIVE

I will look exhausted but pretty when you're done with me.

INSTEAD OF THE half-day shift I expected, my co-worker proved a no-show, and I bagged extra overtime, something I'd appreciate later. The holiday rush didn't manifest, a miracle in my opinion. I thanked every god and goddess I could think of, figuring all of the religions must have gotten together for a respite of that magnitude.

The few customers who did come in wanted to play hardball, a challenge when I ran on fumes.

Somehow, I made it through the day, and rather than having to take public transportation home, another miracle showed up in the form of Jonas and his beloved SUV. He even played the part of a gentleman and opened my door for me.

"When you texted me that you'd be working a full shift, I got worried," he admitted. "We can postpone the park appearance if you'd like. I won't have you prettied up for over an hour."

"We made a deal, and we are going to the park, and I will

play my harp, and I will not get a pity dollar from you, sir. If I earn my pity dollar, it will be on my own merits, thank you."

"I already bought the laptop. I got bored, and I figured if you didn't earn a dollar playing your harp, we could make a payment plan for it like you wanted. The store would've closed before we'd gotten done. I bought the machine on my standards rather than yours, and I asked for some help picking a model a lady would appreciate. It's stylish and works well."

Stylish and works well worked for me. "Are you sure you're not an angel? I always thought you were a devil."

I buckled my seatbelt, and Jonas closed my door before circling his vehicle and getting behind the wheel. "I'm a little bit of heaven and a little bit of hell."

"That you are. Egotistical, too."

"It's part of my charm. Are you really sure you want to do this tonight? You look exhausted."

"I will look exhausted but pretty when you're done with me. It might help me get that dollar I need."

"Okay. I'll let everyone know we're on, then. We have an email thread. They're impressed with your tenacity, at least."

"I was born tenacious. I refused to leave the comfort of my mother's womb for over thirty hours. Honestly, I'm surprised she didn't drown me as an infant for putting her through that."

"I have seen your baby pictures. You were far too cute to drown. Your mother also loves you dearly. I've heard the entire story. Several times. Spare me, please."

"That's something." I stretched my legs with a tired groan. "Uma is damned lucky I like her enough to take over her whole shift."

"Uma should be worshipping the ground you walk on. How was your shift?"

"I think everyone went to late parties last night and were too hungover to go shopping today. The ones who came in, however, were grouchy. So grouchy. I expect the hordes will begin their attacks on their wallets starting tomorrow through the holidays."

Jonas snorted and drove in the direction of my apartment. "You're probably right. It helps Halloween fell during the work week this year. Had today been Saturday, you would've been screwed."

"Fridays are usually bad enough, but I think you're right about the hangovers. I feel hungover, and I only had a glass of sparkling wine. I needed that glass because of your sister. I *needed* it."

"Saw her dressed up as an inflatable dinosaur and decided only alcohol would get you through the night?"

"Precisely."

"You're incredible."

"No, I'm stupid for agreeing to attend that damned party."

"It wasn't that bad." Jonas grimaced. "Okay, it was that bad. It's the first time I ever skipped a party in fear of watching my sister's best friend meltdown because of an asshole man. When someone like you begs a complete stranger for an out like that, it's bad. Really bad. Also, I had no idea you could reach that level of desperation."

"I came to the party with that as my game plan because I just knew it would be bad. I was expecting worse, but honestly, that didn't happen only because I had a date with zombies instead."

"That sounds better than a date with a gay guy."

"Dates with gay guys are the best. They don't expect

anything other than a conversation and a good time, and I don't mean the kind of good time where only one person enjoys what happens in bed."

"Under normal circumstances, I'd feel compelled to defend my gender, but after last night, I'm just going to nod, smile, and agree with you. I'm a lot of things, but I'm not stupid enough to assume 'not all men' will help in the slightest. Because talking down at you doesn't help. You probably get a lot of men like that, don't you?"

"I have a strict policy about men now. No ring, no late-night extracurricular activities. The ring also comes with an expectation of marriage, preferably a set wedding date, a plan for the future, and solid evidence of commitment."

"That sounds surprisingly traditional and conservative."

"It's neither. It's a reflection of the fact I'm tired of little boys dressed in men's clothing wanting in my panties. The no-ring policy ensures I don't have to deal with that. I have a battery-operated boyfriend, and we have a good relationship."

Jonas huffed. "That was an overshare, Lee."

"But a necessary one. Like, seriously. Who has time for little boys dressed in men's clothing? If I wanted to be a mother, I'd get married and have kids. Or adopt, not that I can afford the fees *or* a kid. I really can't afford a kid. That is another reason for the no-ring policy. The no-ring policy prevents children I can't afford."

"Ah. I see. It's not conservative or traditional. It's terrifyingly sensible and practical."

"Exactly. My budget would break if I attempted to add another living being to it. It wouldn't just break, it would shatter. I definitely cannot afford any children."

"Not with an extra twenty or thirty a pay. I'm going to

have to be very careful about who I introduce you to. A woman who understands how a budget works is a rare and special thing. My sister? She views budgets as general guidelines that her credit cards permit her to violate at will. And then she expects Mom to help pay off the bills when she finds she exceeded her general guidelines. Mom, being Mom, ultimately pays them. Yelling at my sister does no good, as she is above anything as mundane as a scolding from Mom."

"How about you?"

"I'm not quite as bad. I try to limit parental bailouts to once a year at absolute most." Jonas patted the steering wheel of his baby. "I shamelessly begged Mom for help with this acquisition, but unlike my sister, I promised to help run errands and use my vehicle for her benefit. That won me my precious."

"Who picked you up to fetch your SUV anyway?"

"Mom. I told her about the period gown, and she decided she had to help. Unfortunately, there's an issue."

Uh oh. "What issue?"

"Juliette was over at Mom's place when I called. She overheard the period gown conversation. I vaguely heard something about revenge would be coming in the background. She might show up at the park, but she won't wreck your performance at least. She might give you ninety-nine cents, though. She's evil like that."

"I can't tell if I love her or hate her. She rolled on my feet, Jonas. She hugged my legs. I'm not certain, but I'm pretty sure she cuddled with the hem of my Prada."

"If she doesn't give you ninety-nine cents, I would not be surprised if she found the same dress in your size and showed up with it. Sometimes, revenge for her comes in the form of a gift. Or, if you're really unlucky, she'll kidnap you."

"She'll *what?*"

"Kidnap you. She's a repeat offender, but for some reason, no one ever presses charges. Mom's gotten grabbed twice so far. In a year. This year, actually. Both hostage situations lasted about thirty hours, which is the average amount of time it takes for Juliette to do a wardrobe revamp for sizing, dressings, and experiments. Don't tell anyone I said this, but Mom goes out of her way to be snatched."

"Is your entire family crazy?"

"I'm waiting for my chance to be kidnapped, but she doesn't snatch men often. I'm considering begging."

"But what if I miss work because I was kidnapped?"

"Juliette is a considerate kidnapper. She waits for days off or finds a way to send in a temporary to cover the hours of her victim. She tends to meticulously research her targets. I suspect that has something to do with her dodging charges. If you don't want to be kidnapped, you have to directly tell her you are unavailable for a kidnapping."

"Shouldn't people always be unavailable for a kidnapping? We're talking about kidnapping here."

"Juliette is not a sane human being. She's a wonderful human being. She's generous and wears her heart on her sleeve, but she is not a sane human being. She wants to change the world, and she doesn't know how to do it for everyone, so she kidnaps people and changes their world for a while because it keeps her from feeling like a failure."

"Are we talking about the same woman here? Juliette Carter, the fashion designer, who headlines fashion magazines often, feels like a *failure?*"

Jonas shrugged, pulled onto my street, and got lucky, finding a parking spot outside of my apartment building.

"Are you sure you want to go to the park? You look exhausted."

"I play the harp better when I'm too tired to think. I will play even if it kills me. And I'll get my dollar because my playing will be so awful people pay me to stop."

"It didn't occur to me people might pay you to stop, and this makes me glad I got bored and already bought the laptop for you. Also, I have news for you."

I got out of Jonas's SUV and narrowed my eyes. He got out, shut his door, and locked the vehicle.

He stared at me. I glared back. "What news? It better not be bad news."

"There was a mouse in your apartment. We ran into each other in your kitchen. As such, if Juliette doesn't kidnap you first, I am, and I'm going to move you into my condominium in secret. We won't tell my family, as they will be jealous, but I can't leave you in a mouse-infested apartment. Also, there was a package for you. As I was afraid the mouse might damage the package, I have the package in the back."

I had some bad news for Jonas. "That wasn't a mouse. He's a rat, and I've seen him before. As long as he stays out of my instruments, I don't care he's there. It's not like I've had any luck getting rid of him. He's too smart for the traps. Well, maybe there's more than one of them." There was definitely more than one of them, but they usually stayed in the walls where they belonged without bothering me much.

"You've been checking their sex?"

"I have decided they're all male rats, as I refuse to accept they are breeding in the walls."

"Move out or be moved out. Decide. I think I'm going to take you to the park after dressing you in that damned period gown, then we're coming back here, and we'll pack my SUV with your most important stuff, and I'll hire a mover to get the rest into storage or my condo."

"That won't work, Jonas. I work here, remember? You live in Manhattan."

"I bet I could find you a job at a good boutique near my place. You'll get better pay and free rent. It'll be my good deed that'll last for however long you take over my spare room."

"No, Jonas. The rats in the wall are fine."

"They are not fine. One ran over my damned foot!"

For fuck's sake. "It's just a rat."

"It's not just a rat. It's a disease-carrying death trap with fur and teeth. It will rip your throat out in your sleep, just you wait and see."

"If a rat rips my throat out, I won't be able to see because I'll be dead."

"You can't stay there."

Where had the asshole Jonas gone? Had announcing his status as a gay man somehow flipped the asshole switch to the off position? I couldn't handle a non-asshole Jonas. Asshole Jonas would've shrugged and let it go. "Can we talk about this after you make me pretty and dress me in a nice gown, so I look like a lady from a painting?"

"I will make you live at Mom's house. That's close to your work, and someone would drive you to work, I'm sure."

There was only one thing worse than moving back in with my parents: moving into my best friend's parents' house. "I would rather knock on the rat's nest and ask if I could move in with them first. That's worse than moving back home, Jonas."

"Your mom would love it. Mine would love it even more. Actually, they'd both love it if you moved in with either one, really. It gives them excuses to visit each other often."

"No."

"Temporarily? Long enough for me to get an exterminator in there? I can't deal with knowing you're living in a rat-infested apartment building."

"I think you're blowing this way out of proportion."

"I am not. There are rats in there." Jonas drew in a deep breath and straightened his shoulders. "But, I will leave it alone until after you have been transformed into a beauty rivaling those painted ladies you like so much."

It would have to do for the moment. "Take pictures. For some reason, I don't think this will ever happen again."

"I'd bet against you on this one, but you'd find some way to get even more out of me, and you're the damned most stubborn woman I've met in my life."

"Juliette Carter, your mother, your sister, and my mother exist, and you've met them, Jonas."

"And you are their queen, they just haven't realized it yet."

I rolled my eyes and headed to my apartment. Dealing with rats seemed a lot easier than trying to convince Jonas just how wrong he was.

THE PACKAGE, from an anonymous sender with a taste in art similar to the Penthouse Guy, contained two framed paintings, one depicting a wintry landscape while the other went the more traditional flowers route, with the blooms held within an elaborate vase staged on a wooden surface.

I would lose hours studying the details of both. Before I allowed Jonas to work with my hair or dress me up, I hung them on the wall so they wouldn't be ruined by any inter-loping rodents.

"I see where I stand compared to those, a rather distant third," Jonas announced.

"I'm attributing these to the Penthouse Guy, and he's on notice for being too generous."

"I understand why you might suspect my friend."

"Well, I had plugged my address into his phone, so he's the most likely suspect. I haven't figured out why he'd do such a thing, but I've decided I don't care. My walls finally have paintings. Paintings that I like a lot." I pointed at the wintry image, depicting a snow-covered landscape waiting for spring. "That one is my favorite."

"After watching you at my friend's place, I would've thought the flowers would've been your favorite."

I smiled, tracing my fingers along the patterned frame of the winter scene's painting. "The flowers are lovely, and they're very stereotypical of Renaissance art, this one is different. I don't think it's Renaissance; the colors and tones aren't right for it, but it's still beautiful. If anything, it's more beautiful because it's focused on hidden potentials. I love paintings like this, where it's all about the potential of the future. The landscapes wait for spring, and who knows what lurks beneath the snow?"

"Will we have to check in on you every now and then to make sure you haven't starved to death admiring your new paintings?"

"As a matter of fact, yes."

"I'm going to turn you into a lady fit for a painting now, so I don't have to think about the possibility of you staring at some paintings until you starve to death."

With a startling amount of cursing and two bottles of

hair spray, Jonas transformed my hair into black roses and decorated his work of art with sparkling bobbles and trinkets, the kind I often saw in boutiques but could never justify getting for myself. He raided my jewelry box, grunted at the meager selection, and went for my single string of pearls. "I know what to tell Mom to get you for Christmas now."

"No."

"You're losing this one. I have been recruited to be this year's present informant, so you're just going to have to deal with it. At least you have matching earrings. Do you regret the dress yet?"

Before I'd gotten into the dress, I'd believed they were like modern dresses. I'd believed dressing would be a simple affair.

No.

I'd been wrong. It had taken Jonas almost an hour to lace me into the damned thing, and he'd about suffocated me in the process. I understood why the ladies in the paintings I liked never played wind instruments. How had they breathed?

I missed breathing.

"I do not regret the dress," I lied. "I question why you tied it so tight my voice has gone up an entire octave."

"You only squeaked once, and that was during the initial lacing. This is how the dresses were worn, and to make you authentic, I had to put you in an authentic dress. This is as authentic as it gets."

"What era is this from, anyway?"

"I asked for a Renaissance dress to transform you into a painted beauty. This is the dress I was given after telling the seamstress your size and showing her your picture. The hairstyle is modern, but I wouldn't know how to do the hairstyles from the paintings even with the help of a manual. I could figure it out, but it would take more time than we have. Under no circumstances are you to ask where I acquired the slippers."

The slippers made me unreasonably sad. If I could, I'd wear them every day for the rest of my life. "They treat my feet so well, Jonas."

"I'm sorry, but you can't keep the slippers. If I could give them to you, I would."

"It's okay. They probably cost more than I can afford anyway."

"So, you said you were going to play the harp. Where is this harp?"

The dress made moving interesting, as the laces essentially paralyzed my upper body. I'd be able to play the harp, although I questioned how women from the Renaissance period had survived daily life. I went to my closet and grabbed the harp's case from the upper shelf, amazed I managed to get the damned thing up there in the first place, considering how much it weighed. "If they get into my instruments, Jonas, I will torch this building to the ground."

"But will you move in with my mother until I can figure out how to deal with the rat problem?"

I considered it. "Maybe. The rat problem would be solved, though. The building would be a pile of rubble and ash."

"Okay. Here's our new deal. Should any of the rats damage any of your instruments, I will help you replace or repair the damaged instrument, and you will move in with my mother until the rat problem can be dealt with—without an act of arson being committed."

"Fire is the only way to be sure."

"Lee, arson is a criminal offense."

"It would be worth it. Do you have any idea how hard it was for me to get some of those instruments?"

"I'm concerned I'm underestimating the situation here."

"That's because people with money don't get what it's like to be a person without money." I opened the harp case and pulled my prized instrument out, carefully setting it on its base. The harp came up to my hip, and had it been made of a heavier wood, I doubted I would've been able to lug it around in a case at all. "When I bought this, it was damaged, and my parents, particularly my mother, saved up so she could have it restored and repaired. I'm pretty sure she did work on the side with the restorer to be able to afford it. I called around and asked, and it was hundreds of dollars neither one of us had. You may touch it, but you may not damage it in any way, and I will remove your fucking fingers from your hand if you touch the strings. You do not get to fuck with my harp."

Jonas held up his hands in surrender. "Even I can recognize when a woman means business. I won't touch the harp. It's a pretty instrument. Do I want to ask how much you paid for it and where you got it?"

"I got it from a pawnshop for fifty dollars. It was in pretty bad shape when I bought it, but all the strings were intact, and it still worked somewhat. I think the guy at the pawnshop paid five dollars for it; it was in such bad condition."

"How much could you sell it for now?"

"It turns out the pawnshop guy's an idiot and didn't know what he had. The restoration work wasn't cheap because the cords had to be specially made to match the harp; it's pretty old, but it was treated acceptably. It just had an awful amount of surface grime. At some point in its past, someone had done some treatments on it to protect the wood, which saved the instrument."

"I can't help but notice it looks... rather plain."

I understood Jonas's hesitation. To all appearances, there wasn't anything special about my harp, which was a little too large to sit on my lap but too small to be treated as a proper full-sized harp. It had seen a lot of years, and it was a little like me: it didn't fit in really anywhere. If anything, it looked ready to give out its last breath and die on me. "It's Gaelic, and it's about four hundred years old."

"And you got it for fifty dollars?" Jonas jumped back, and he shook his head. "You were about to hand me an ancient artifact! I could've dropped it. It looks heavy."

I definitely got exercise picking it up, and I risked giving myself a concussion every time I shoved it onto the extra-wide shelf, which barely had enough space for it.

I loved my harp, but it wasn't a great instrument to carry anywhere, and if I'd been smart or wise, I would've made a stand to give it some height and put it in a permanent spot in my apartment.

"The original strings survived the abuse, which is how the restorer was able to get a reading done on the metal alloy used, the gauge, and construction of the wires. They're as close as we can get to what the harp originally had. I have the original strings, but they're no longer on the instrument. I worry they'll snap the instant someone tries to play using them. That's why the pawnshop guy sold it so cheap. He didn't want to pay for it to be authenticated, I guess. Mom had it authenticated."

"Do I want to know how much that harp is worth?"

"Probably not."

To the right buyer, I supposed it could fetch a pretty

penny; the artist's name and date were carved into the base, hidden beneath decades of grime, which the restorer had removed to return the instrument to its former glory. "This instrument is my true treasure of the lot, but every instrument I have has a story."

"I feel like I've underestimated you."

I returned the harp to its case and closed it before fetching the rest of my instruments and checking them. I introduced Jonas to each one, and he figured out where I'd gotten them all after the fourth.

"Really, Lee? You spend your free time and money browsing pawnshops looking for instruments?"

"Yes. And I try to play them, too. But I like the harp best. I suck at the reed instruments."

"Maybe you should try blowing instead of sucking. That might help."

"You, sir, are still an asshole," I muttered.

"I didn't want you to forget about my asshole tendencies."

"Well, thank you for the reminder."

"Is this all of them?" Jonas counted instruments littering my bed. "You have twelve here."

"The ukulele is in the living room with the harmonica, and the clarinet hides behind the couch with the saxophone." I triple checked all my instruments to confirm rats hadn't gotten into them and returned them to the closet. I put the harmonica away in its proper place on the lowest shelf with my reed instruments. "It doesn't appear I need to burn the building down yet, as the rats have wisely stayed out of my important possessions."

"I'll beg, Lee. Please move in with my mother for at least long enough for me to get an exterminator in here to get rid of the rats."

"It wouldn't help. They'd just gnaw their way back in after a few weeks. That's what's happened the few times the landlord has tried to get rid of them. There could be worse things in the walls, anyway."

"Like what? Snakes?"

"Flying cockroaches."

Jonas shuddered. "I'm just going to grab your new laptop and its bag, and it's coming with me, because with my damned luck, a rat will pee on it, and then your new laptop would be ruined, you will become upset, and you might light the building on fire."

As rats had peed on my clothes before, I worried he made a good point. "How about this? I'll think about it—and start looking for a slightly better place if I can afford it."

"Mom has a lovely guest room she'd love to rent to you for a pittance, and she'd even open up one of her project rooms to give your instruments a proper place to live. It's not a free handout if you're paying rent, nor does it count as living with your parents. You'd have to deal with my parents as landlords, but you wouldn't have rats."

"I'll consider it."

"That's better than a no. Shall we go to the park, Your Majesty?"

"I'm not a queen, Jonas. I'm a pauper."

"You may not be a queen, but you sure as hell look like one right now. And, I have to admit, I'm damned curious to see how well you play the harp."

I sighed. "I'm going to need my stool."

"Your stool?"

After triple checking my harp case was firmly closed, I walked into my living room and pointed at the stool I used when I played my harp, which served double duty as a general junk stand. "Just toss the stuff on the couch. That's where I sit when I play my harp. It's the right height."

Jonas did as asked, but rather than tossing everything, he transferred everything with care. "How long did it take you to find this?"

"I didn't find it. I made it."

"You *what?*" Jonas stared at my stool. "You made this?"

"I asked around until I found someone with a wood-working shop. I needed a stool, and he taught me how to make it and supplied the wood. I helped clean up around his shop in exchange, and I play my harp for him sometimes."

"I almost regret I have zero interest in women, as that is absolutely incredible. I think I finally understand what my mother sees in you. And my sister. And my father. Life hasn't given you jack shit, but you make it happen anyway, don't you?"

"I prefer to think of myself as too damned stupid to quit."

"You're not stupid."

I looked him in the eyes, arched a brow, and replied, "I just argued with you for how long about refusing to move out of a rat-infested apartment, why?"

"Right. Because of pride. Okay. I can accept that you're too damned stupid to quit. That said, I'm exchanging stupid for another word in my head."

Frowning, I considered him. "What word?"

"Tenacious."

I doubted I would ever understand my best friend's brother.

SIX

I regret this already.

WHEN I THOUGHT of going to a park, I thought of Liberty State Park, as I enjoyed the view of the Statue of Liberty across the water. Jonas had decided to drive through crazy traffic to Paterson Great Falls National Historical Park. For ambiance, the park scored a lot of points with me. I loved everything about the place. Waterfalls soothed me, reminding me there was more to life than just going to and from work.

I'd never played my harp at a waterfall before, and I could think of a lot of songs that would do the place justice. As my level of exhaustion bordered on critical, I'd settle for some more classic melodies, as I'd played them so many times my fingers didn't require any input from me beyond the initial notes.

To my dismay, the park was busy for so close to closing time, and the lot itself lacked any spots at all, requiring us to park along a nearby street with a bunch of other people. "How many did you invite?"

"Technically, I only invited ten, and all of them are people you've met before or I'm related to. That said, I told them to recruit bodies for you, but to recruit nice bodies for you."

"I regret this already. I better earn a dollar, Jonas. I need that laptop, and I've earned that laptop. I'm dressed like a lady from a painting with an old harp, it's no longer Halloween, and now I'm going to be the comedy highlight of the hour."

"You'll be fine. Neither Mom nor I would invite anyone nasty to something like this, and we might be rich, elitist snobs, but we enjoy outings to the park as much as the next person. And most of us enjoy live entertainment."

"I look like an idiot."

"You look like a beauty who deserves to be in a painting. I did a fantastic job of dolling you up. Strut your stuff with pride."

"I might get the slippers wet."

"Don't worry about the slippers. The owner of the slippers and the dress is aware they're being worn into a park. If she can't get the grass stains out, that's her problem, not yours."

"Grass stains are the worst."

"Then it's a good thing it's not your problem." Jonas grabbed my stool, tucked it under his arm, and pulled out a picnic blanket from the back of his SUV. "My mother thinks I'm crazy for keeping a blanket in the back, but I don't want your stool to get damaged, and this will spare the slippers and the dress from additional harm."

As I'd been planning on resting the harp's base on my foot to protect it from the grass, I'd appreciate the blanket once it was time to play. "Thank you."

Jonas pointed to the vantage overlooking the waterfall.

"There's a nice spot by the water a little farther down. If you're shy, unless you're that good or that bad, people will leave you alone. It requires effort to move."

"If they're willing to drive all the way here from places like Manhattan, is there any chance of them being lazy?"

"Now that they are out of their cars, the weather is nice, albeit cold, and they are enjoying the view? Definitely. I love being lazy. Lazy is a true art form, not those poser paintings you like so much."

"They are not poser paintings, and I will join forces with your sister to make you pay for all eternity if you do not put a dollar in my harp case to go along with my new laptop."

"You are not assertive often, but when you are assertive, I learn the true meaning of fear."

Lugging my harp across the park drew an unfortunate amount of attention. The instrument ensured I couldn't move faster than a snail's pace, especially while waging war against the layers of skirts I wore. "The next time I ask to be dressed like a lady in a painting, remind me ladies in those paintings wear a billion pounds of clothing."

"If you were wearing a billion pounds of clothing, you'd be flatter than a pancake. Do you want me to carry the harp?"

"It's not that far. I can do it." I might plunge into the water, but I'd drop the harp first. The case would protect it; I'd made sure the case could survive the apocalypse while guarding its precious cargo.

The spot Jonas picked would work, and he spread out the blanket and set the stool down for me while I dug out my harp from the case along with my tuner. While I could tune by ear, if I screwed my first string up, I'd screw all of them up. Prepared to wage war with the old instrument, I sat down and checked every string. Only a few required adjustments, much to my relief.

In the time it took me to tune the instrument, I'd gained a crowd, and Jonas's mother waved at me, grinning from ear to ear while Juliette Carter arched a brow.

She held a black bag, and I figured she could cram a body —mine—into its depths without any issues. "Hey, Jonas?"

"Considering you just engaged Juliette in a staring match, I'm not sure I want to hear this question."

"She brought a body bag with her. How do you think she's going to kill me?"

"In the garden with a rope, obviously. Rope is the closest she can get to thread, and she'd never use her sewing scissors for a murder. She might attempt to murder anyone who uses her sewing scissors for anything other than fabric, though."

"There is nothing worse than someone using your good fabric scissors on anything other than fabric. The blades have to be perfectly sharp, or you can ruin the cloth."

"I would not let Juliette Carter know you actually know your way around a sewing machine or fabric scissors."

"She already knows, Jonas. That's why she's out for revenge. She knows I'm the one who butchered my Prada."

"Well, you have an audience. I'll try to keep her from murdering you, but no promises. I'm amazing, but I can't perform miracles."

"If you see your sister, drown her. This is all her fault."

"My sister is working tonight until late, as it seems she has to pay her way for once in her life."

"What an absolute tragedy."

"Isn't it, though?"

With my luck, Jonas would tell his mother there were rats in my apartment, Juliette Carter would overhear, and I'd be the latest kidnapping victim unwilling to file charges, as who in their right mind wouldn't want to be treated like a doll by a fashion designer? Well, outside of those with a firm grip on reality and basic common sense.

As I'd gone willingly to a park while dressed in a Renaissance gown, I possessed a weak grip on reality at best, and common sense wasn't as common as the name implied, so I wouldn't beat myself up over my lack of. Instead, I'd play my harp, do my best to ignore the crowd, and be happy I could play with an audience for a rare change.

Movement out of the corner of my eye, at the fringe of the crowd, drew my attention, and to my dismay, I recognized Jonas's friend, the probable sender of my new paintings, and the owner of priceless pieces of art I'd treasure if given an opportunity to move in with him.

Well, it made figuring out what to play easy. I'd rotate through the classics and serenade the man's collection and toss in some lamenting ballads about what wasn't meant to be. I thought the music did a fair job of representing life and humans in general.

We always wanted what we couldn't have.

MY LACK of a social life and general obsession with musical perfection prevented me from making a complete fool out of myself. While I didn't play anywhere near my usual standard, the harp made up for it. Compared to modern harps, it had a unique tone, something that spoke of its age and gave its music a haunting quality. When the restorer had finally finished, he'd cursed those who'd kept the instrument alive for so long while allowing it to decay, and he'd marveled how something so precious had turned up in a pawnshop.

I thought I had a lot left to learn about—and from—my harp.

I played ten songs before my fingers protested playing. The crowd applauded, evidence I wasn't the only lunatic in the park. Stretching my hands helped ease some of the strain, but I recognized when it'd be foolish to continue. Exhaustion would reduce me to a blithering mess within an hour, and I wouldn't even care where I slept.

"Done?" Jonas asked, striding over. "You look exhausted."

"I am definitely exhausted. Your penthouse buddy showed up."

"He heard I was dressing you up like a porn star, so he wanted to see what a gay man thought a porn star looked like."

Some in the crowd snickered, and I wondered how long Jonas had kept his secret before losing any care about what others thought about his sexuality. One day, I might understand—maybe.

No, I probably wouldn't, thinking on it. As far as I was concerned, it was business as usual with a few bonuses.

"And he showed up?"

"I did say it would be porn he'd probably like."

The crowd, which already began to disperse, lacked Manhattan's best kisser, much to my disappointment. "For all I know, he's probably the actual porn star, and I kissed him, which means I'm going to need to be tested for whatever diseases I might pick up from kissing strangers. I bet I could entertain myself for hours looking for how I'm going to die on the internet."

I went to put my harp back in its case only to discover a

problem. It contained a wide variety of stuff, including the laptop bag with my new treasure in it. Triumphant over having bested my best friend's brother, I pointed at the prized dollar bill sticking out from under the body bag Juliette had been carrying. "I might be dead by dawn, but there's my dollar, which means I win."

"That would be my mother's contribution, as I'd foolishly told her about the wager."

I set the harp aside, careful to keep from knocking it over, and checked the body bag.

Empty.

"It's really a body bag, Jonas." I considered the bag and the oddities in my harp case. A brand-new phone, still in shrinkwrap, stood out as among one of the more sensible pieces. "Someone put a phone in my harp case. A new one. A really nice new one."

"I told everyone that our bet was for cash. It was determined anything that wasn't cash was fair game."

I grabbed the phone, which proved to be a rather high-end model, the kind I dreamed of. "Isn't this really expensive?"

"Well, you're not slacking in the phone department now. I'm glad I didn't hold back on the laptop, or that phone would've put my efforts to shame." Jonas crouched next to my case and poked around the wealth of presents. "Whatever you do, don't ask about the purse, use it happily, and don't think about its brand." To make it clear he intended for me to use the purse, he took my new phone away and put it inside. After some more digging, he held up a bag and laughed. "This must have come from my sister."

Within the bag was a pair of red-soled heels so tall I could use them as weapons. "She got me hooker heels?"

"In her opinion, every woman needs a pair of hooker heels. I disagree with her, but I have learned not to question her enjoyment of hooker heels."

"Why do you think Clarissa is responsible for those shoes?"

"They're her favorite pair but in your size. She keeps them on her nightstand, and she pets them. I walked in on her once, and it scarred me for life."

I giggled over the thought of my best friend cuddling with a pair of shoes before bed. "She would, too."

Setting the shoes aside, Jonas rummaged, piling various bath and body products I'd enjoy making friends with to one side along with a bunch of hair accessories. Then he stumbled across a rather large blue box. I recognized it as coming from Tiffany and Co, and my eyes widened. "That can't be."

"I'm so jealous right now," Jonas muttered, prying off the lid. He tilted the box to catch the fading sunlight. A round necklace encrusted with red and clear stones accompanied a matching tennis bracelet, a pair of earrings, and a ring I might mistake for an engagement band if I hadn't known better. "There's a laptop ridiculous, a phone ridiculous, and then there's this."

"But why? All I did was play the harp for a while. I didn't even play all that well. I can get your sister. She's crazy. But the rest of this? Why? Who would do such a thing?"

Jonas shrugged, his expression so bewildered I believed he hadn't been involved with the appearance of the jewelry. "I have absolutely no idea. I mean, I know why I bought the laptop. You're nice, you work hard, and you just don't get anywhere. Although I misjudged you a lot. You could teach me a thing or two about turning trash into treasures. We'd just buy the latest and greatest. You took something nobody else wanted, and you made it into something special. That harp of yours is something special."

"If you like antiques, yes."

"No. It's the sound. I've heard harps before. We rich bastards love status symbols. Harps make excellent status symbols. Yours sounds nothing like the ones we use."

"It sounds like a harp, Jonas."

Jonas snorted and returned to sorting the items in my harp case. "Some classical art prints, probably from the Penthouse Guy, a copy of the zombie game, probably from the Penthouse Guy, although several people are aware how much you like that game, and gift cards for various stores and boutiques. Ah-ha. Maybe you were right about the body bag theory." He held up one of the gift cards. "This is a rather aggressive note disguised as a gift card. Well, it's a gift card, but it's the terrifying kind."

"It's from Juliette Carter, isn't it?"

"It is, and while you can run, you can't hide, and if you put up a good fight, she'd appreciate it. She signed with her name."

"What's the gift card for?"

"A pair of running shoes and an appropriate outfit to go with them. From her brand." Jonas checked inside the card, and he laughed. "The card itself is actually a tracking number for a package. I have some bad news, though."

"She has the address for my work?" I guessed.

"She has the address to your work."

"I'm calling in on my new phone, and I'm quitting. I will quit, Jonas. After I quit, I will run away. If I don't, she'll show up at work and ruin me. Forever."

"It doesn't work that way, Lee."

"It doesn't?"

"She doesn't break careers. She makes them."

I shivered. "Why does that sound like a threat?"

"Because when she's involved, it really is. If you move in with Mom, she might not be able to get to you quite as quickly."

Jonas's mother, who waited not far away and undoubtedly heard her son's comment, waved at me.

I bowed my head and wondered if prayer might save me. "Who should I pray to for deliverance, Jonas?"

"I don't think even prayer will help you at this point, but good luck trying."

Damn.

WITH JONAS and his mother hot on my heels, I entered my apartment to discover an entire swarm of rats holding a party in my kitchen. I could only assume something had driven the furry, disease-carrying bastards out of their nest and into my home.

"I'm going to burn the entire building down now," I announced. I kept a pack of matches and two lighters in my bathroom. I had everything I needed to purify my apartment with flames.

I made it two steps before Jonas wrapped his arm around my waist, grunted, and lifted me off my feet. He transported me to the hallway and set me down beside his mother. "I could deal with one rat. I cannot deal with an entire family of rats. Mother, don't let her escape. I'm going to rescue her instruments, we are going to put them in our vehicles, and we are leaving. If you don't take her home, I'm taking her home. If she's lucky, she'll meet Tommy."

"Tommy?"

"One of my boyfriends."

"Wait. One of your boyfriends? How many boyfriends do you have?" I couldn't even get a boyfriend, although I was more-or-less at fault for that. "Did you step out of the closet into a gay utopia?"

"I'm stealing that and making it mine. I'm rich, I'm beautiful, and I'm sexy. All the men want me." To make it clear he would win no matter what I did, he flicked imaginary hair over his shoulder. "I inherited my mother's charms."

"It disgusts me that I have to admit he's right on that score. I'm sorry, Shirley. He's in a mood today. Do make sure you fetch her some clothes, Jonas."

"I refuse. What if a rat peed on them?"

I groaned and bowed my head. "I'm going to be homeless by the end of the day, and I'll be okay with that because I don't think I want to renew my lease now. Technically, it will be a month and a day, as I'm required to give them thirty days' notice. My lease renews in a week. I don't think I want to renew my lease."

I wanted to cry, as I could handle one or two rats, but I'd seen the writhing pile of rat bodies taking over my kitchen. They would wait until I slept, and then they'd infect me with every rat-induced disease known to man. If they couldn't infect me, the fleas they surely carried would. Dying from so many diseases would make the headlines, and I would unseat Florida Man as the crowned champion of terrible ends. I would single-handedly prove Darwin's theory.

"Jonas, darling, please just retrieve her instruments before she has a breakdown in the hallway. It wouldn't do to ruin her pretty makeup. We need to take pictures."

"Pictures?"

"I didn't get sufficiently beautiful pictures of you today." Without any evidence she worried about the rats, the woman swept into my apartment. "Where are the instruments? I'll help."

"Check behind the couch, Mom. Make sure those two paintings on the wall come with us, too."

As the pair would rampage through my apartment if I left them unsupervised, I joined in, helping to gather my precious instruments and new paintings.

In the time I had gone, one of the little furry bastards had chewed on my saxophone case and had peed on my harmonica. Nothing would save the harmonica, as there was no way I'd purify it enough to my standards. I would replace the saxophone case, but the instrument had escaped unscathed.

Fury led to hyperventilation, and I flexed my hands, debating how best to light the building on fire. "I need my matches, Jonas. I need my matches, a few gallons of gasoline, and a few more matches, just to make sure the damned thing ignites. I will burn this whole city to the damned ground."

"I will take you pawnshop trolling for a new harmonica myself, and I will see if there's anything we can do to fix the case."

"I have to put my mouth on that. There is no fixing that harmonica. I am not putting my mouth on something rat pee touched. No. I need my matches, Jonas."

"There's hysterical, and then there's homicidal," my second mother announced, and she went in the kitchen long enough to find a plastic bag. She opened it. "Put it in here, Jonas."

The harmonica went into the bag, which she sealed. "If you want to light it on fire, you may do so at my house in the fire pit. I won't provide gallons of gasoline, but I do have some lighter fluid you're more than welcome to."

"They peed on my harmonica."

"At least it wasn't the harp. I think the saxophone case can be repaired, but if not, I'll replace it."

"The case is a piece of shit that deserves to be lit on fire, too. It might be diseased. It burns. With fire."

"By default, fire is required to make things burn."

"Acid burns things without fire," I reminded him.

"I draw the line at acid." Jonas counted instruments, muttered curses, and began ferrying them to his SUV, leaving me with his mother.

"You're just having quite the day, aren't you?"

"I'm dressed up like a Renaissance hussy, I played a harp badly in the park, and rats peed on my harmonica. Add in that I got barely a wink of sleep last night, and we've graduated from quite the day to I want to get out of this day like a bat out of hell. Maybe I should fetch my Prada." I sucked in a breath, my eyes widening as I realized I'd hung the dress on the lower rail, which put it in easy reach of rats. Darting back into my apartment, I went to the closet, opened the door, and discovered a second swarm of rats.

Somehow, they'd pulled my Prada from its hanger, and what was left of it formed a nest.

All I could do was take a picture. I even used my new phone to do it.

"Jonas? We have a situation," his mother called out, and she patted my shoulder. "It'll be okay."

"Juliette Carter is already out for my blood. When she finds out what happened to the dress, she's going to be out for more than blood."

"But it won't be your blood. Also, as I noticed you took a

picture, send it to me, and I will send it to her. The explosion will be spectacular, and I wouldn't miss it for the world. With her, you can either play the game or get steamrolled. If you can't beat her, have fun with her."

"Are you suggesting I should have fun with a crazy stalker?"

"She's only a little crazy, and if you ask her to stop, she will. She doesn't make a good stalker, as she cares too much about her targets. You'll get used to it."

"I will?"

"You'll be living at my house. It's inevitable. Also, I can't wait to tell your mother I've finally acquired you as mine and mine alone. Now, please let's get out of here before I faint, scream, or both. Those rats look angry."

I closed the closet door to contain the nest long enough for us to make our escape. "And possibly hungry."

"Definitely hungry. They ate your Prada. But, that said, they have good taste."

JONAS and his mother had a spectacular fight in her driveway over who was keeping me. As I couldn't handle any more insanity, I went into the house, hauling my harp with me. My second father, who often joined in the ongoing dispute with my actual parents, met me at the door.

"You look lovely, you also look exhausted, and I'm willing to bet no one thought to feed you, so I have done my fatherly duties and put a frozen pizza in the oven. It'll be ready in ten minutes. Consider Clarissa's closet yours, so steal what you want. I won't tell if you don't, and it's not like my wretched little girl bothers visiting often since she got hooked up with a place of her own."

"I heard that Dad!" my best friend shrieked from the direction of the living room. "If Shirley is living here, I'm living here, too. I'll pay rent."

"No."

"Dad, don't you be mean."

"Your apartment doesn't have rats, so you don't get to move back in with us. We just successfully got rid of you. Stay gone. Visit no more than two nights a week."

I laughed at his harsh affection for his daughter, who really was a hellion on a good day. "I'm sorry to intrude."

"The rats ate your Prada and ruined one of your instruments. It's not an intrusion, but as I know full well you won't accept charity, I'm charging you rent, and we'll draw up a lease in a few days. We'll pick something fair that lets you start a savings account for yourself, and we'll help you find an arrangement you're happy with that doesn't involve you sharing space with pests. Non-negotiable. I already spoke to your parents about the situation."

Shit. I was a dead woman. My mother hated rats more than anything else, and Dad, technically my stepfather, didn't like them either. Mom would invade while Dad would shake his head and brace for the insanity of my mother on the warpath. "She's coming over, isn't she?"

"No. She's hitting a pawnshop looking for a new harmonica for you. Also, I believe part of your rent will involve you taking us to pawnshops to experience this for ourselves. Your harp is an amazing instrument. Actually, I'm impressed the wood's integrity survived enough it can still be played. I could hear its age."

"The restorer did a lot of work on it."

"I need their contact information if that's all right with you. I know people with old instruments they want restored, and that harp is a masterpiece. I also will discuss how much you were charged versus how much you should have been charged."

Damn, my second father was on a roll. "I feel like I have four angry parents out for my blood today."

"We're not after your blood. We are out for your apartment, however. The wife said you're up for lease renewal next week?"

Damn, damn, damn. "I am, and the lease papers are with me. Jonas was afraid I really might try to burn down the building."

"I wouldn't blame you if you did, and I would pay for your attorney."

"You're a very strange second father."

"Thank you for noticing. I hope you like meat on your pizza, as it seems we only keep pizzas for carnivores in the house."

Clarissa bounced into the entry and pointed in my direction. "You really do look like a lady from a painting!"

"Your brother did the makeup and got the dress."

"For once in his life, he is cool. Why is he yelling at Mom in the driveway?"

"They're fighting over where I will live for the next while."

Snickering, Clarissa leaned through the door and shouted, "Mom wins because Mom actually likes Shirley. Stop being an idiot, Jonas."

"I like Lee just fine, you heel-obsessed freak."

"That is just a low blow, and I resent the accuracy of your jab."

"You should know better than to yell at me. I always win."

My best friend grunted, flipped her middle finger at her brother, and stormed inside.

Huh. "What's wrong?"

"You're not moving in with her, I suspect."

That made sense, and I sighed. "It's not like I asked to be moved, Clarissa. They decided for me. The rats decided for me, that is. They ate my Prada."

My best friend returned, and she crossed her arms. "Tell Dad he has to let me move back in."

"You enjoy your personal freedom and ability to sleep with anyone when you want and how you want without your parents offering critiques. Remind yourself of this until you realize I'm not actually a winner of this situation."

"I should be hurt, offended, and disturbed by that statement, but it's all true," my second father admitted. "And please don't tell me anything about who you are sleeping with. I raised you to be independent, and I don't want to be tempted to have a talk with any of your boyfriends about how they should be treating you. If they aren't treating you properly, we'll be having words about it—and I will need bail money."

"Dad, it's fine. And I'm currently single. But I do have a few candidates I might attempt to lure into my lair. As my lair would be rather restricted, I will add this to the con column of my list. But sharing a roof with Shirley is really high on my pro column."

"I would charge you twice the rent of what you normally pay trying to recoup some of the investments I sank into you."

"I would like to withdraw my interest in moving back in despite Shirley's presence."

"I'll be a nice father and say you can visit three nights a week, but you can't bring a man over unless you're planning on marrying him."

"I find your terms acceptable, and I accept your generous offer." As wise women retreated in the face of unbeatable odds, Clarissa backed away. "I'm going to keep an eye on the pizzas, as I don't want to be the reason Shirley really does turn into a mass-murdering lunatic."

"When have I ever been at any risk of becoming a mass-murdering lunatic?"

"You tried to set your entire apartment building on fire to kill some rats. So, tonight. Other people do live in the building," my second father replied.

Huh. "You're right. I think I need to go get out of this dress, eat some pizza, and go to bed. I've never been so happy to go to work before in my life. Work seems normal. Also, I have no idea how I'm getting to work tomorrow, and this is a problem."

"I'm driving you, and I'll pick you up, too. We'll see about fixing your car situation, as well."

"Taking the bus is a lot cheaper than a car."

"Be that as it may, the nearest bus stop is almost a mile away, as my wife really liked this house and this house has an allergy to buses."

"I'm still trying to figure out how you found the only place in Jersey without an accessible bus stop."

"Snobby rich people syndrome. Why put in a bus stop in a place where most people won't use it? We're rich and snobby, Shirley. That's how being rich and snobby works. That, plus the last time I took a bus, it reminded me what having an infant was like, except it was adults losing control of their bodily functions. It left scars."

Having used the subways, buses, and trains in the area the entirety of my adult life, I understood and I'd seen far worse. "I recommend against taking public transit if you can avoid it."

"You do have your driver's license, right?"

"Despite not having driven a vehicle in a few years, I do have a valid license."

"You're driving yourself to and from work, and you will deal with me in full hover parent mode while I make certain you remember the key points of how to drive."

I couldn't win, and having seen the cars the entire family-owned, I would spend the entire drive in utter terror of scratching their beloved vehicles. "There's crazy, then there's letting me drive your car crazy."

"You get to choose between the Porsche and the Audi. I've decided the Land Rover is not nearly flashy enough for your refresher course in driving."

"I can't drive a manual."

"We're taking the Porsche, and you will be learning. Clarissa!"

"Hold on, the pizza's almost done," my best friend screeched from the kitchen.

"But that's your Porsche."

"It has a dual transmission system and a manual paddle system, and it's the friendliest of my cars for teaching the finer points of driving a manual. You'll pick it up with no problem."

Jonas and his mother came in, still bickering over my living arrangements.

"Jonas, she's staying here, as I've been informed she hasn't driven a car in several years. You're unqualified to give her a vehicular refresher course, and I'll be forcing her to drive my

Porsche to and from work until I'm satisfied she is qualified to use her license."

"I lose," Jonas announced. "The Porsche is fun. You'll like it, and well, I can't top that, and I drive an automatic. I'm a lazy driver who doesn't care about my mileage. I also love my baby, and I'm not sure I could bear the thought of you driving through Manhattan in it. Me driving it around Manhattan is terrifying enough."

"Manhattan is terrifying, period," I muttered. "You lost just because you decided to live in Manhattan."

"It has its perks. My boyfriends love living with me because I have a great location to go with my great ass."

I shuddered at the thought of Jonas using his home as his love shack. "Just how many boyfriends are living with you right now?"

"Permanently, none. Frequently? A few."

"Can I have a fraction of your luck? Really, just one boyfriend would be nice."

"Don't announce you're in the market for a boyfriend right now, Lee. You dressed up like a lady and played the harp where the parents of a lot of eligible bachelors could see you. You might not be wealthy, but you're officially cultured, and despite our crazy, money-spending ways, we like cultured. You'll be a prized target if it's discovered you're on the market."

"You have lost your mind, Jonas."

"I have not. You already have a secret admirer."

The only admirer I wanted shared my love of art and had likely delivered two paintings for my enjoyment for no reason other than he could. "I do?"

My second parents glared at their son. "She does?" they

asked, their tones so accusatory I covered my mouth so I wouldn't start laughing."

"Someone gave her a Tiffany set. A ruby and diamond set. Then there was a set of classic art prints in her harp case and the two paintings that showed up at her apartment while she was at work. She also got some really nice gifts for playing her harp."

"First, it's not my fault rich people are crazy and put stuff in my harp case. Also, just because the stones are either red or clear does not mean they're ruby or diamond," I announced.

"Lee, it's from Tiffany. It's a ruby and diamond set."

"He's right," my second mother said, shaking her head. "I didn't see anyone add a Tiffany box to the case, though."

"It was buried under other things, so whoever did it may have added other things to the pile or recruited help. I'm concerned, though. Juliette left an empty clothing bag in there. Lee thought it was a body bag."

"In my defense, it's black, it's big, and it looks like it could fit a body. She also swore revenge. Death would be revenge. Now she's going to want extra revenge because of what the rats did to my Prada."

My poor Prada. I hoped it rested in peace despite being the nesting ground of rats.

Jonas shook his head. "It would leak."

"Pizza's done!" Clarissa called from the kitchen.

I abandoned the insanity for dinner, and I'd hope to hell I didn't get anything on the dress, as I was too damned hungry to change before indulging in hot, cheesy goodness.

SEVEN

I had to admire the woman's cunning and ruthlessness.

HELL WAITED for me at work the next morning, and it didn't take long for me to determine Juliette Carter had begun her campaign for revenge. One of her higher-ranked employees invaded the boutique with an offer only an idiot in the fashion world could refuse.

With a catch.

In exchange for including the boutique in a new line launch, at her standard rate, which most boutiques viewed as a steal, Juliette Carter would come to the boutique in person, pick an employee, and train said employee to her satisfaction to handle the launch. Then, since that wasn't bad enough, the chosen employee would have to wear some of the new clothes and pose for interested customers.

My manager looked ready to cry from joy, as the owner would be thrilled with such an offer. Fashion line launches could make a boutique and drive new customers to it for weeks. To make the launch too good to refuse, Juliette Carter wanted it for the week after Thanksgiving, beginning on Black Friday.

I read the writing on the wall.

Juliette Carter would get her hands on me, and she'd use my employer and the holiday shopping season to do her dirty work. Once she had her hands on me, she would take me for all I was worth.

I had to admire the woman's cunning and ruthlessness.

To make matters worse, Juliette's employee was still at the boutique, poking his nose around everywhere to get a feel for the place.

I considered quitting. Quitting would work. I could escape reality. I could start hitchhiking across the United States to somewhere saner. I could pack up my harp and play for money until I reached California. According to most television shows I'd seen, most places in California seemed pretty nice even during the winter. I could escape the snow, the slush, the sleet, and the New Yorkers for paradise.

I could handle being broke in California just as well as I could in New Jersey.

I went through the motions, did my best to ignore Juliette's employee, and tried to make sure I got to every new customer first to prevent anyone from trying to drag me into the insanity.

"Shirley, do you have a moment?" my boss asked after I handed off my latest customer to the cashier.

Damn it. I needed to figure out how to play ball with a fashion designer, but I recognized the bitter truth: I was in way over my head. I was so in over my head that hitchhiking to California with an ancient harp seemed like a really good idea. "Ma'am?"

Since running away wouldn't work, I walked over, doing my best to ignore the man in the suit that would make a huge mess of my day if he picked me.

No, *when* he picked me.

Juliette Carter would somehow pay for bringing her madness to my day job.

"Clifford is going to be coordinating the Carter brand launch. I want you to work with him to make certain everything goes smoothly. You've been in line for a promotion to management anyway, so this will be a good chance to see if you've actually learned anything while on the job."

It would have been nice to know I'd been in line for a promotion of any sort, but anyone wanting to put *me* in a management position needed to have their head examined. Also, the last time someone had gotten 'promoted' to management, it had involved chaos and torture, and the poor bastard had quit after a week.

The boutique's owner liked getting rid of people during the transition process, cutting hours while they learned how to be managers. "Management?"

Our boutique had two managers, and my boss was one of them. The other manager had just survived the promotion process, although she only worked when the main manager, my boss, couldn't come in.

"I'm resigning at the end of the summer, as I'll be going to design school full time. You're the current candidate to take my place."

Since telling her hell no and to kindly go screw herself with a stick would get me fired, I tried to find a silver lining in the cloud. Increased pay? No. No amount of money on Earth could make up for working management at the boutique. On a good day, the most I could hope for was making an unhappy customer somewhat pleased with my service. The holy grail of nice customers came by once a month at the absolute most, and I rejoiced when they showed up.

I'd heard rumors from other retail slaves about promotions to management. Managers dealt with the worst of the worst, and they were expected to smile the entire time. They had to dress better, too, and I doubted my boss's paycheck made up for the heightened clothing bills.

At least I could come up with a polite answer that might please the woman. "Congratulations on going to design school. Which one?"

"I'm going to London. I figure it's time for a change of pace, and they have a nice design school over there. It isn't Parsons, but I've been talking with admissions, and I'll be starting in the fall."

"That's great." When I went to my temporary home, I would retreat to my room, crawl beneath the bed, and hide. Possibly for all eternity. I liked that I could hide beneath the bed, but I worried what anyone would do if they caught me hiding down there. "What do you want me to do?"

"I want you to figure out who should be on shift for the Black Friday week. I doubt we can get authorizations to bring in extra bodies, so we'll have to be as efficient as possible. The Carter corporation will provide some staff for the event to help oversee sales of its product line. They'll need to be trained on our software and registers. You'll be in charge of this."

"Understood. I can put together a list of the other employees who would work best in which jobs, and how to split the shifts for the week before starting inquiries on Monday."

"Monday will work. Clifford will give you his card, and you can work with him to figure out how many Carter employees we'll need for the event. They're used to working with small boutiques. I'll cover the floor while you coordinate with him. If you need help, fetch me."

I wanted to raise my fist at the woman, but I smiled and nodded instead, waiting for her to leave before bucking up and preparing to deal with Clifford. I wouldn't view him as the enemy. Yet.

"I have a message for you, Shirley."

"I've already been kidnapped by another adult I'm not related to, so I'm going to kindly turn down any invitations to be kidnapped. My quotas for being moved to someone else's home have been met for a while. Also, rats ate my Prada, and I probably deserve what Juliette is going to do to me, but if she could give me a few days to process that a swarm of rats broke into my apartment, picked my Prada for their nest, and completely destroyed it, I would really appreciate it. It took me years to save up for that dress, and now it belongs to a bunch of rats. Someone also bought me a Tiffany set, and I'm not sure what to do about that, either. A few extra days would be nice. Then there's the phone and the other things I found in my harp case. Really, I'm going to need at least a year at this point."

Clifford raised a brow, but after a moment, he chuckled. "You've had an eventful time of it lately. I'll let Juliette know. The message, however, I'll still pass on, as you may find it interesting. In addition to the message, I've been told that you're to know I am but one of her many minions."

Wow. The woman really called her employees minions? I

opted to ignore that element of the insanity. It would take time to accept Juliette called her employees minions. Acceptance would involve acknowledging I would never be interesting enough to call anyone beneath me a minion, even if I did get a job promotion. "Is it a *good* interesting or a *terrifying* interesting? Personally, I found Psycho to be a very interesting movie, but I wouldn't want to be cast in it. That's the terrifying interesting. The good interesting involves turning back time so I could rescue my poor Prada."

"She wanted me to let you know that she will plot her revenge and come for you only after the other party is finished with you first. She also wanted me to thank you for your excellent entertainment last night, but she is concerned you're not getting enough sleep."

"Well, that's my fault. I played video games at a hot guy's house with a gay friend until the wee hours of the morning, then I went to work because I won't skip work for being stupid. I deserved to look like hell. But, just to be clear, I'm not going to be kidnapped today?"

"You're not going to be kidnapped today."

"Stalked?"

"You're definitely going to be stalked today, but I promise she's a really polite stalker. She really does mean well, and she will stop if her stalking at all bothers you. Mostly, her version of stalking involves showing up in a public place, usually armed with a favorite beverage. Her targets are usually enticed into spending time with her due to the lure of the beverage and her wickedly nice ways. She's a very open and friendly stalker."

"That sounds like what friends do, except slightly creepier."

"We've come to the conclusion Juliette believes she is

very bad at making friends, has found something she thinks works for her, and has embraced it with full enthusiasm. In reality, she is exceptionally good at making friends, but she doesn't agree with us no matter how many times we explain this to her."

"Let me get this straight. This woman wants to be friends with me, so she's going to stalk me with bribes of my favorite drinks?"

"That sounds about right. She has other methods, but I think she's going to go the stalking with favored beverages route this time. She can be very unpredictable, and she tries to plan her attempts at making friends with her target in mind."

"Is she a really good person or a really bad person, Clifford? I'm getting mixed signals. Also, I like black tea with a little bit of sugar and cream. I also enjoy chai. If a chai, I like extra nutmeg and cinnamon sprinkled on top. I like chai more than black tea, but black tea is my usual."

"She's quite a lovely person, but she's a little crazy—in a good way. She's very nice and she cares a lot. She's not like other CEOs." Clifford made a note on his phone. "I'll make sure she knows what drinks you like so she can properly indulge in her stalking tendencies."

I ignored that Clifford was serving as Juliette's informant, as she'd find some other way to figure out my favorite drinks even without her employee's assistance. "She's not like other CEOs?"

"She takes a limited cut from her designs and work. Don't get me wrong, she's definitely wealthy, but she isn't one of those billionaires thriving off the backs of her minions. She chooses to be paid less so we can be paid more, and she lets us fight over who gets to work overtime. She offers very good overtime incentives."

"Do I want to know? Or will I end up feeling sorry for myself while working the boutique scene?"

"She saw what you did to your dress, ma'am. Do not be surprised if you're kidnapped one day with the intent of her luring you into working for her. She's always looking for talent and courage, and it takes a lot of both to alter a perfect Prada and come up with something even better. She really liked what you did with the dress. Frankly, she treated it as a job interview. Honestly? She sent me here to bring you back with me, but unlike her, I'm sensible, and you're not the kind to abandon your responsibilities to your employer. With you coordinating the line launch, she'll restrain herself until after the holiday season."

"But don't you all work in Manhattan?"

"We do."

I sighed, my shoulders slumping. "I can't afford Manhattan."

"You can afford Manhattan; you just don't know it yet. I'm originally from Philly, and I laughed in her face when she suggested I should move near the main offices. Who can afford that, right?"

I nodded. "Right."

"Any one of her employees can, comfortably."

"Even customer service?" I asked. "Does she have customer service? I assume she must. She works with clients, right?" Customer service always got the short end of the stick. I'd done a stint in customer service before working full retail. I'd exchanged one type of hell for another, but at least my retail hell came with a slight chance of a bonus if I helped to sell enough product.

"We all take turns doing customer service, actually. We don't have a specific customer service department. We all do at least five days a month working the customer service lines and emails. Juliette wants us all to stay in touch with our clients, and that means interacting with them at all stages of their relationship with us."

My mouth dropped open. "*Everyone* works customer service?"

"Even Juliette, but we only let her do two or three days a month, and we make her do it when she's frustrated with something. It relaxes her."

"Juliette works customer service? At her own company? She finds customer service work *relaxing*?"

Life no longer made sense to me, and I wanted to go to my new home and hide under the bed for a few days. Hiding under the bed might help. No, I doubted anything would help.

Someone had given me a Tiffany set, Tiffany meant expensive, and I had no idea who would do such a thing or why.

My concerns about the crazy fashion designer came second to the crazy person who had given me something from Tiffany and Co. When I considered and prioritized my situation, I figured the gift giver took the top spot, leaving Juliette as a distant second. "And Juliette is aware of this other person? The one who left the Tiffany box in my harp case? Do you know about this at all?"

"Yes."

Well, if it meant getting some information on what was going on and why, I'd become Clifford's best friend and make sure the clothing launch went well despite everything. Unless she hired me. If she hired me, then I would have a whole new world of options to explore. The way Clifford talked about his job and his boss, I would have secured the Holy Grail of employment. "And this other party is acceptable to Juliette?"

"The last time I checked, she was contemplating how she could use a pair of handcuffs to streamline the progression of your situation, as she believes it would take divine intervention to resolve matters in a timely fashion. She's very impatient to have her turn."

I frowned at that. A pair of handcuffs? Why would she...?

The alternative use of handcuffs came to mind, and I had a certain candidate I wouldn't mind using a pair of handcuffs on. He, however, struck me as a reasonable human being. I'd somehow fallen in with a lot of unreasonable human beings. That decided me. I would be a bastion of sanity in a world gone mad.

I would transform chaos to order. I would make the boutique shine in the face of insane adversity. I'd earn that promotion, even while worried about my ability to tame the chaos surrounding Juliette Carter. "So, the owner of the Tiffany box and its contents is a man?"

"No, you're the owner of the Tiffany box and its contents. The individual who left the box and its contents for you is a man.

"And do *you* know of this man?"

"I am acquainted with him."

Getting a straight answer out of Clifford would take work, and I bet he kept his answers short and sweet to drive me as crazy as his boss. I would not go crazy. I would be calm and bring order. I would not accept defeat at Juliette's hands. It took me a moment to rethink my approach, and I straightened my back and prepared to wage a new type of war with Juliette's employee.

Anything worth doing was worth doing well, and I would not lose. I'd lost enough lately.

My poor Prada. I would miss it dearly. I would not miss my apartment or the rats now residing within it, but I would miss my Prada.

"If you had a daughter, would you allow her to date this man?" I'd discovered rather young if I wanted to know a man's true opinion of another man, I'd ask that question. The answer almost always changed.

Most men didn't want their daughters dating creeps.

"If I had a daughter, and she was interested in this man, I would begin planning the wedding myself. Juliette does not involve herself with matchmaking unless she feels both individuals are good people. She would never knowingly establish a relationship with anyone she views as an abuser. But, I do know him sufficiently to be comfortable with the idea of my daughter, if I had one, marrying him. That is a little more serious than dating, but yes. He's ethical but awkward. Of course, I don't have a daughter, so this is entirely theoretical."

I could work with ethical but awkward. "What does it say about me that I feel like I'm being set up on a blind date, but since it's being vetted by numerous people, this might not be a complete disaster in the making?"

"Being lonely is hard," Clifford replied. "Juliette doesn't like when people are lonely. There has been plenty of discussion of the hallway incident, too."

Crap. "I owe that bastard a kick in the groin."

Clifford grimaced. "Which bastard?"

"Well, not the one I violated with his permission. He's not a bastard. He was quite the gentleman considering the circumstances, really." His mouth had left a mark or two on me, and I wanted a repeat occurrence without the creeper involved. "No, I mean the one that drove me into asking a stranger if he minded being violated. And I also don't mean Jonas. Actually, he deserves a prize right now, since I only picked his friend because Jonas tries to avoid being friends with complete assholes. Jonas can be a jerk, but he's basically a demented brother at this point. A girl just doesn't kick her demented brother in the groin unless he *really* deserves it. He hasn't done anything to deserve it."

Damn. I already failed at being the calmer of chaos, as I babbled worse than a brook.

"Well, I can't say I disagree with you, although I'd prefer another method, personally."

"And I can't say I blame you on that score. I'm just saying, if he tries another stunt like that on me, I very well may do that, and some kind soul should probably warn him he shouldn't get within twenty feet of me in the future."

"I believe I can pass that message along through some trustworthy individuals."

"I could just make Jonas deal with him." As far as threats went, I believed that one to be particularly potent. As I'd already made a fool of myself and interrogated Juliette's minion, taking it a step further wouldn't make the situation worse. While I could've asked Jonas to pass a message to his friend, Clifford seemed like the safer option. "I don't suppose you could pass another message for me, could you?"

"It entirely depends on who is receiving the message."

"Please ask the gentleman I violated if he'd like to have a coffee, he's on the list of people permitted to toss me into the back of his car and cart me off somewhere for a drink or a nice vacation. Actually, a nice vacation from my life sounds ideal."

"I'm not sure who that is," Clifford confessed.

"Just make Jonas tell you. If you grab him by his ankle, turn him upside down, and shake him a few times, he might even have some pocket change. And you can tell him it was courtesy of me. I can't be too nice to the demented brother-like man. He might start thinking I actually like him."

He laughed. "I'll pass on turning Jonas upside down and shaking him for his pocket change, but I'll talk to him about the situation and pass on the message."

"And if you ask Jonas to pass on the message, tell him if he makes a fuss about it, I'll shake him for his pocket change —or make him dress me up again, but this time, like a queen rather than just a painting lady. And I'll make him buy me a new, full-sized harp. Actually, no. I'll make him troll pawn-shops for a full-sized harp. That'll teach the bastard."

"I'll make sure he makes a fuss about it," Clifford promised.

Damn. Were all minions of crazy rich designer ladies nice? If they were, I'd have to do some serious thinking about flinging myself under Juliette's thumb. "Does it make me a shameless hussy that I'm hoping he puts up a fight and obeys my verdict?"

"I saw a recording of you playing your harp. I might turn him upside down and shake him for his change if he doesn't put up a fuss and participate in trolling pawnshops for one for you. But, I would like to ask, why not ask for a new one?"

"I like the ones that need some tender loving care and have a history."

When I wasn't trying to hide it behind a shield of false

bravado, I wanted some tender loving care, and I came with a history, too.

"I am going to do you a favor," Clifford admitted.

"What?"

"I'm not going to tell Juliette you're okay with being kidnapped if the goal is to have a date with somebody. That is how you get kidnapped before you go on a date with somebody. Juliette will never, ever say no to planning a kidnapping when the kidnapped party expresses any sort of interest in being kidnapped."

"Does it make me a bad person if I confess he's gorgeous, he has good taste in art, and he's quite possibly the best kisser in Manhattan? I mean, can you really blame me at that point?"

Clifford took his time thinking about that. "I find it disturbing that I'd think about inviting myself to a kidnapping under those circumstances."

"Oh, well. A girl can dream, right?"

"You're dealing with Juliette Carter. She's in the business of turning dreams into reality."

"Okay, then. I want a hot date in the entry of his penthouse underneath his Leonardo da Vinci sketch. Clothing optional. Wait, no. Clothing is only optional if we have a wedding date, plans in progress, and so on. I have a line, and only those I'm engaged to with an actual expectation of longevity get a piece of this package at this stage in my life." Damn it, I'd overshared. "I should not have told you that."

"You're having a stressful day, and it's completely normal for stressed individuals to blurt what's on their mind. I've heard worse."

"You have?"

"You should've been there for the time the boutique

owner freaked out because she'd had bad sex in the spot where Juliette wanted to set up a mannequin. That incident was priceless."

"Oh my."

"That's what Juliette said, and as she didn't want to deal with that disaster, she moved the mannequin to the other side of the store. She then, for the peace of the boutique owner's mind, got some bleach, then a rug, and then moved a rather heavy display case over the spot. They burned some sage, too."

"Sage? Why?"

"I think they were attempting to drive away evil spirits."

"I thought that was salt."

Clifford shrugged. "I wouldn't have a clue, but the boutique's owner was desperate and willing to try anything to exorcise that bad memory. So, on the scale of things I've heard setting up these events? That was barely a blip on the radar."

"If I get to that stage preparing for this event, all that stuff I said about not being kidnapped? Ignore it and proceed with a kidnapping. Preferably to somewhere with nice water, a beach, and an art museum within easy walking distance. I'll even put up with Juliette to escape at that point."

"It's always good to acknowledge you have limits and come up with a plan on what to do should you reach those limits."

I nodded my agreement, heaved a sigh, and asked, "What do we need to get done to make this event happen? For some reason, I have the feeling this is going to get a lot worse before it gets better."

"I have a binder. We're going to need some space, and I

recommend you take pictures for later reference. If you have a tablet, that will streamline the process."

I didn't, but I'd make do with my new phone. "I'll tell the boss I need to skip out to handle planning for this. We don't have much space for spreading out paperwork, and there's a coffee shop down the street. I don't know about you, but I could use a drink right about now."

I'd just ignore spending some of my hard-earned money on a luxury while facing the fires of hell in the form of planning an event at the boutique.

EIGHT

Is this a kidnapping or just a coffee date?

IT TOOK the rest of the day to go through Clifford's binder and get a better idea of the mayhem that would be unleashed on the boutique when Juliette Carter came with her clothes. To sell the prospect to the boutique owners, Clifford had statistic sheets for sales for both successful runs and flops. The flops were few and far between, and at worst, the boutiques broke even on their investment on the day of the event.

The numbers staggered me. In some cases, the event sold out of the new line, which meant no one else could place any orders or take home one of the new dresses, suits, shoes, or other accessories up for sale. While one or two items were the star, the boutique had the option to carry excess from other events that hadn't entirely sold out for a set markup.

I appreciated that Juliette Carter set rules on pricing and wouldn't allow her clothing to be deeply discounted. The contract forbade such discounting without her permission, and she would not accept a lower cut to give any boutique an edge in the market.

Once Clifford left, insisting I keep the binder so I could make sense of the madness, I questioned my life. If my boss had seen the binder and the strict list of requirements boutiques needed to meet or exceed to remain eligible for the event, I hated her for dumping it on my shoulders. I didn't even care if she thought I could take over her job.

Organizing the event was so over my pay grade that I wanted to take the binder and shove it right up her ass before quitting.

I'd put some serious thought into quitting—after the event.

Two could play at being evil bitches, and while I wouldn't completely screw my employer over, I wouldn't be taking over my boss's job, not without the sort of pay raise to make it worth my while. I understood the system: I'd be expected to work extra hours to make the event happen without a hitch, and I'd be expected to do it on my time. Unpaid. My manager *might* authorize overtime for the event.

If she didn't, I expected my frayed patience would snap.

Armed with the binder, I returned to work to find everything quiet. My manager pounced the instant I returned. "How did it go?"

"It went fine. We have a lot of planning work to do to make sure we stay eligible for the event, and the owner will need to review the stocking options. You, or the owner, will need to get on the phone with them to figure out how much extra merchandise you'll want to bring in. The binder has the rates for everything, the risk assessments, and everything else needed to make a decision on it. We'll need to give the designer an answer on stock in a week."

She snatched the binder out of my hand, turned on a heel, and marched for her office. "You're done for today. We'll talk more tomorrow."

I checked the time, which revealed I still had three hours left of my shift, and since I wasn't a salaried employee, it meant unless I got called in for overtime, I ran the risk of being dropped to part-time status. If I dropped to part-time status, I would no longer be eligible for benefits when the enrollment window came up closer to the end of the year. It'd been written in the fine print that the employer held the rights to transition full-time employees to part-time at their discretion. If they meant to cut my hours by fifty percent, they'd have to give me written notice, but I rarely worked more than thirty to thirty-five hours a week except during the holidays, which meant they could bump me below thirty hours into part-time without any notice.

It wouldn't take much to lower my average to below thirty hours.

As a part-timer, I would still get limited benefits, but I'd kiss my health insurance goodbye along with a few of the other perks full-time employees enjoyed, including the discounts I rarely used.

Shit, shit, shit.

I didn't want to think about my insurance, which already cost me too much. I already couldn't afford a cold, let alone a more serious condition. I focused on my more immediate problem. What the hell was I supposed to do for three hours?

Beyond catch a bus and walk the hefty distance to my new residence, I had no idea. I checked to make sure I had everything, clocked out, and left.

Juliette Carter hadn't waited long before making her first move, and she held two beverages in her hands. "I have brought chai to lure you into a vehicle with me, and I can ask a minion to cover your work if needed."

Damn. I'd have to thank Clifford for the warning, but I'd have to have a talk with him about wasting no time telling the evil woman my secrets. "I was cut loose early today." I eyed the drink in her hand, decided the risk of being kidnapped was worth it, and accepted her offer before claiming my drink. "Insurance renewal is coming soon, so they're adjusting hours."

"I've heard that story before. Dropping you to part-time, probably aiming for an average of twenty-nine hours, so they don't have to give any benefits? Twenty-nine hours per employee, with a few extra employees added to help carry the load. Then, they'll juggle the schedule to make sure the hours look inconsistent to prevent labor groups from nailing them on planning such a thing in the first place, despite employers having the right to do just that if they please. They don't even have to juggle the schedule since it's completely legal. And most boutiques don't have labor unions helping to secure better work conditions or rights."

"Sounds about right. It's the first time I've had hours cut this openly, though. I'd been maintaining full-time since I started working for them." Granted, I grabbed every extra hour I could, sliding in overtime during unexpected outings. Most at the boutique just lived with either part-time or trying to push for full-time hours.

At last count, the boutique had four full-time employees, myself and my manager included.

"They'll probably bring in a handful of new employees for the event, pick the best, and move them up in pay scale or position, but they'll test the waters on everyone part-time to help mitigate the cost of the event. I wish I could block boutiques from doing that, but I can't legally mandate how they handle their employees during preparation or during the event. I can just mandate how many of their employees are on the floor to make sure the event works properly; if they can't provide the number of employees needed to handle the load, I can't run the event. I've been doing this long enough to know just how many trained staff members we need."

"Is this a kidnapping or just a coffee date? I feel I should establish general expectations moving forward." I sipped the chai to find it made exactly as I'd described to Clifford. "This drink has elevated you to my list of people who can participate in a short-term kidnapping today. The list has two people on it right now."

"I assume the other person is the gentleman you had an engagement with at the party?"

"Not Jonas."

"Not Jonas," Juliette replied, her tone amused. "I hadn't been planning a kidnapping for today, but I'm always game for an unscheduled kidnapping. The SUV is mine, get in it, and I shall begin your kidnapping."

I never understood why the wealthy often drove sporty cars or SUVs, but I got into the vehicle as directed. "I'm only doing this because Clifford told me you're a friendly crazy person rather than just a crazy person."

"Clifford is an excellent minion. Clifford is also a single minion, and it is only a matter of time until I locate a lady worthy of him. She'll have to be extra special, however, as Clifford has some special needs."

"He does?"

"He keeps snakes, which he loves more than life itself. So, his future bride must love snakes. It's very hard finding a single woman who loves—or even tolerates—snakes. It will be a challenge, but I look forward to it. Now that he works at the main headquarters, I can begin my work with him in earnest."

I wondered if I should warn Clifford, then I questioned why I was getting into a car with Juliette, and I decided I would sip my chai and hope for the best. "You're a chronic matchmaker, I see."

"That didn't take you long to figure out."

"I'm just going to warn you directly that I do not participate in evening activities with any man unless I'm engaged to him, as I have already had my fair share of assholes just wanting sex, which significantly cuts down on the pool of men willing to put up with me the instant they learn they won't be putting a pawnshop ring on my finger, getting sex, and then wandering off. If they want the goods, they have to be in for the long haul."

"Well, I appreciate your directness. My other targets usually just run away screaming, try to hide, or do what I want while utterly clueless I'm helping them secure long-term happiness."

"Well, you are a little crazy, Juliette."

"Only a little?"

"I was trying to be polite."

Juliette waited until I got into her SUV and closed the door before circling the vehicle and getting behind the wheel. She stabbed the lock button on her door. "Your kidnapping has now begun. You cannot escape me."

Sometimes, when someone told me I couldn't do something, I did it to establish that I most certainly could. When I did this, I looked my target in the eyes while I did it.

I pressed the unlock button on my door, and the vehicle

obeyed my command. "I, too, have the power to lock and unlock doors." I pressed the button. "Now it's a hijacking, and I have kidnapped you. I'm just permitting you to drive so I don't get a second charge of car theft."

"I have been kidnapping people for years, and you are the first to challenge me. But fair is fair. I accept your terms. Where are you taking me?"

"I want evidence you are actually half as nice as people keep telling me. Clifford mentioned you wanted to hire me."

"I only employ full-time people. I do not maintain at-will rights, and should an employee be terminated for any terminable offenses, short of immediate firing offenses, we are required to attempt to fix the problem. I do not like firing employees, but I have some rules that must be followed."

"Criminal activity being one of them?"

"Correct. We don't condone illegal activities. In the case of drug abuse, should the employee seek help, we cover their rehab and other medical expenses and have our own program. Drug use happens. I don't fire an employee over it. I don't even require a drug test for hire, but I do require all employees to attend informational sessions on mental illness and drug abuse. You don't have any of the common signs of a drug abuser."

"I considered becoming a raging alcoholic when I found that rats had pulled down my Prada and shredded it for a nest," I confessed.

"When I received word and photographs of the dress's state, I tried to drink straight from the bottle. My husband took the alcohol away until he saw the picture of the dress. I was allowed to have half a shot. I am planning revenge. On the rats, not you. You've been punished enough. Mostly."

"So, my first task is for you to drive me to your offices, explain what you could possibly want someone like me to do at your company, and, if possible, show me others who work in the same position."

"I see you have embraced the idea of taking control of your life with great enthusiasm."

"And yours, as I've carjacked you. I can point my finger at you in a threatening fashion if you would like."

"I love it best when my targets have lost their desire to withstand corporate abuse. It's so much fun watching them try to take over the world. Or at least take over their situation. I've been told your living situation is less than ideal."

"I have zero prospects, I lost three hours today when I can't afford to lose any hours during a pay period, and the only reason those lost hours aren't going to result in me eating dry noodles for a while is because my second parents would not allow me to even think about skimping on food. My second parents can be scary."

"I have arrangements with some landlords in the area of my office buildings. My employees adhere to certain rules, but we control the rent to keep it reasonable. They get continuous business and assurance their tenants are employed and can pay their rent, and my employees can have comfortable lifestyles. I can't house all of my employees, but those who aren't in the upper parts of the company are taken care of. The ones who are paid more can afford their fancy pads."

"I'd be at the lower end of the tier. I'm used to that."

"Darling, you redesigned the perfect Prada into a perfect witch's costume. You're going into design, and my designers are paid exceptionally well. What I will do is draw the base design for new clothes, and you will take what I do and turn them into something marketable. I'll then do more work to refine the design, and that's what is manufactured."

"I know nothing about design, Juliette."

"Perfect. If I wanted to hire some fool who knows the current fashion world, I'd go steal employees from design school. If you can't draw, I will teach you how to draw. If you can't draw even after lessons, you will sew the design and someone else will draw it. I already know you can sew. Your work on the Prada showed that. The belt was excellent, and I may have you work accessories. I don't work as much on the accessories as I should, so I always need clever people who take my boring belts and turn them into interesting belts. But I am involved in every design that has my name on it."

"I'm not sure this is how it should work."

"I'm positive it's not how it should work, but at my company, that is exactly how it does work. You'll get used to it."

I recognized her tone. Juliette held full confidence I would get used to it, had zero doubt I would be in her employ, and she'd make sure I got used to it—and liked it in the process. While I'd technically carjacked her, I worried she'd already won the battle and the war at the price of being bossed around for a short period of time.

"Will anyone miss you while you're kidnapping me and taking me to my own office building?"

"One of my second parents is expecting to pick me up from work, as he is not convinced I can drive a vehicle safely. He wants me to get in more practice."

"Can't practice driving when you don't own a vehicle."

Well, I appreciated that she understood my situation. "Exactly."

"Do you even want a vehicle?"

"Not particularly."

"You like public transit?"

"Like is a strong word, but it is affordable and gets me to where I need to go. I like walking, but that isn't really feasible."

"There's an apartment building a block from the office. I can ask the landlord to reserve the next opening for you. Or I can call in a favor from a friend and ask if you can occupy his residence until my earliest convenience. His place is within walking distance."

"That's not how moving works, Juliette."

"It can be. I am very convincing. I am satisfied you can handle any potential issues associated with living under the same roof with a man."

"If the man in question is Jonas, he is gay, he has already attempted to move me into his place, and I already said no because I would not want to ruin his lifestyle, which involves many men at one time. Honestly, I'm just jealous, as I can't even land one man. I can get why they'd want to be with him. When he's not acting like an asshole, he's a really nice guy."

"Do you have a house key for your second parents' place yet, or will I have to commit an act of breaking and entering?"

"I have a key and a code."

"I recommend you order me to drive you to their place, and we will sneak inside, get a bag packed, and go on an adventure into Manhattan. I make no promises that you will be returned to your place of employment. I'll have Clifford drag in one of the new recruits for some testing."

"Testing?"

"So, I have this infuriating habit of claiming employees for a while. I send in minions to cover their work. It's part of the contract for hosting events with boutiques. I also have arrangements with some shops in case I want to lift one of their employees for a few days."

"And then you poach their employees?"

"If offering a living wage in a different state is sufficient to poach them, then they didn't deserve their employee in the first place. New Jersey is an at-will state, and they do allow employers to set terms for employment within reason. I try to follow the key rules in states nearby, as it helps when I want to poach an employee. I'm totally going to poach you. I'm just figuring out how to bait my trap."

"Honestly, having more than twenty dollars a payday for emergencies and extras is a good start." I shrugged, well aware I'd found rock bottom. "Don't take that as complaining. It's just my situation right now."

"And those three lost hours hurt when you only had twenty to spare to begin with."

"It wouldn't be very hard to poach me right now. My manager claims she wants me to take her position over when she goes to some fancy design school in London, then she cuts out three of my hours after dumping the event on my shoulders."

"There are no rules against being employed by multiple people at one time, and if your job is to go to your other job and make that event work well, this is cost-efficient for me, as there's nothing as frustrating as a failed event. I particularly hate when launches fail because of mismanagement at the boutique." Juliette headed towards the rich part of Jersey, and I worried over how well the woman knew the area. "If you do well with the boutique management, I might put you under Clifford's wing for a while when you aren't learning the art of design. I do like my employees having skills usable throughout the company. Sometimes, designers need a break, so they work the releases, and sometimes the coordinators need to do something artistic. Having a fluid workplace makes this a lot easier. Then there's the issue of settling you in Manhattan."

"Not with Jonas," I insisted. "There is no way I will live with a man who has better luck with men than I do. It would be nightly torture. I've met Jonas's friends. They're hot."

"I try not to torture employees whenever possible."

"Well, that's something. Also, maybe you should know I currently don't own much, although I'd like to pick up my harp and paintings if you're planning on having me for more than a single evening."

"If I have my way, I will be handcuffing you to something solid in your new residence and leaving you there. The cuffs will be the kind the police use and actually require a key to open, leaving you stuck until I feel you will agree to stay there."

"I don't want to be handcuffed to a toilet, and I will not be happy if I'm handcuffed out of reach of a toilet. No handcuffing."

"I could handcuff you to your new roommate."

"No."

"I resent your immediate rejection of my plan to handcuff you."

"Nice people do not handcuff people together."

"I'm not nice today. In fact, I'm quite rude."

I worried I'd be as crazy as her through exposure. "When I met your minion, I swore I'd try to be a bastion of calm in a world gone mad. I feel like I have already broken my promise multiple times since making it."

"That seems like a rather foolish promise to have made, Shirley."

"Can I at least get you to call me Lee? I figure if I have to hitch a ride on the crazy train, I may as well have a name I like."

"Of course, Lee. I'm not driving the right car for the crazy train, though. The right car for the crazy train is sportier, and I'm only allowed to bring it out of storage during the summer."

"That's okay. I'm fine with the crazy train departing from the station at a legal speed."

Juliette laughed. "I don't speed usually. I go with the flow of traffic, and I make way for the idiots who want to get themselves killed. New Jersey, I've noticed, has a lot of idiots."

"They call it the Jersey Slide for a reason. The Jersey Slide is why I hate driving. New York is no better, as they've done their best to steal our patented move."

"I'm pretty sure the Jersey Slide is a nationwide tradition at this point. So, you want your harp and paintings. Is there anything else you'd like?"

"My soul back. I wouldn't mind my Prada, but rats own it now."

"I will include a new perfect black dress as part of your hiring bonus."

My eyes widened. "That's playing hardball, Juliette."

"I know. The perfect black dress also includes the shoes and the purse that go with it. I've been informed you have the jewelry already."

"Do rubies and diamonds go well with a black dress?"

"Exceptionally well."

"I hear you may know something about the giver of that

set. Which, I'm assuming, is so expensive I will have an immediate anxiety attack should I learn of its value."

"Mhmm," the woman replied, turning onto the street leading to my new temporary home.

"Is Clifford the kind to shake down a gay man for his pocket change if he doesn't put up a fuss over something? I feel I have made a mistake that might result in this happening."

"Clifford is pretty gentle, but he might shake somebody down for a good cause. What happened?"

"I asked Clifford to pass a message, and if there were a fuss, I'd make someone go trolling pawnshops for a full-sized harp. Actually, I have more than broken my promise to be the calmer of chaos. I'm spreading it, selfishly."

"You play the harp very well. It seems reasonable for you to want something like a full-sized harp. They're expensive. I've discussed the harp situation with your mother. Your stepfather grunted. I wasn't sure what he meant with that grunt."

I grimaced. "Everyone knows about that now, I guess."

"They also know about the hallway incident, but I wasn't the gossip on that one. I just talked to them about your... partner. Apparently, they're more concerned you picked up some disease kissing a stranger than they are about you kissing a stranger."

"Mom is weird. Dad is weirder. Sometimes, I think the ghost of Dad whispers weirdness into Dad's ear. It may have spread to my second dad's ear, too. Dad was crazy, but he was a good crazy."

The good crazy had helped us all cope with Dad no longer being Dad, especially at the end.

"How many fathers do you have, if you don't mind me asking?"

"Currently, two. Dad is Dad, and the second dad is technically Clarissa's dad. Second Dad is the one convinced I need more driving lessons. Dad got dubbed Dad since Dad would be okay with it even if he were still alive, and I figured Third Dad would hurt his feelings. And, after saying that, I realize it really does sound crazy."

"But sweet. What I'll do is this. We'll go get your harp and anything you need for a few days, plus something I can use as a blindfold. I will then take you to where I think you should stay for a while, while blindfolded."

"Why the blindfold?"

"It'll be fun. More fun for me than for you, but consider it part of your job interview. Tolerating the insane is a critical job skill at my company."

I bet. "Okay. But if I say no, I mean no, and the weird stuff stops."

"That is completely fair. Before I blindfold you, we're going clothing shopping."

"We are?"

"I will include all clothes purchased as part of your hiring bonus. We'll go to thrift stores and low-end boutiques if you'd prefer."

I perked up at the offer of going to thrift stores. "You're actually willing to shop at thrift stores?"

"I donate prototypes to thrift stores often, and I tell the stores they can't mark the dresses up. They have to sell for their lowest price as they do for the same type of article. In exchange, I cut a check to the charity of their choice. That way, I don't support the for-profit chains, people have access to the clothes, and they get the reputation of sometimes having my attire show up in their shop. Everyone's happy. And yes, I require a contract. I've had one store try to mark up the clothing, and let's just say I assigned them my meanest attorney."

"Are you related to your meanest attorney in any fashion?"

Juliette snickered. "No, actually. His name is Claud, and he's the sweetest yet meanest man I've ever met."

"I guess I can't get Claud to deal with the rats, can I?"

"There are other and better ways to deal with the rats. Anyway, Claud would faint. He's terrified of rats. He saw a rat on the street once near the office. We had to take him to the hospital because nobody knew how terrified he was of them, so he hit his head. If we'd known, we might've been able to catch him! He was fine, but he cut a few years off my life with that stunt."

From what little I knew of Juliette Carter, in addition to potentially cutting off a few years of her life, her attorney had fired off all of her protective instincts at the same time. She seemed like the type to have a freak fit if someone in her care had any sort of unexpected health issue. "I gave my apartment to the rats. I probably should've just fainted. Or screamed. Or done something other than closed the closet door, abandoning my ruined dress to its fate."

"Yes. I fully intend to use your rat woes to get my way, but only after we get your harp and paintings and leave them somewhere safe while we shop. I'll have one of my minions grab some prototypes that should fit you, too. They'll be prototypes from outfits they don't think will sell."

"Do you have a lot of those?"

"Unfortunately. Designing is one part skill, one part experimentation, and one part too stupid to know when to quit. So, the failures make good temporary clothes during an emergency. Some of my failures are amazing, but my minions are evil and mean to me often. I'll give you the amazing failures. Maybe you can convince my minions they should be added to a future line."

If I gave her any room to maneuver at all, she'd go overboard, but how was I supposed to rein the crazy woman in? "I feel it's worth mentioning that I'm not an employee yet, and you're supposed to give bonuses to people you've actually interviewed and have a hiring agreement with."

"Oh, I'm hiring you. I'm just evaluating how I'll get away with it. My minions? They seem to think I can't just hire whomever I want when I want. I'll just tack on everything I buy to your hiring bonus. Also, I'm definitely hiring you. There are so many things I can use you for, and I love versatile employees."

"You haven't even seen my resume, Juliette."

"I don't need to see your resume. You worked with Clifford all day, and he fed me intel when you weren't looking. Clifford has a good eye. And he said you were obviously intelligent and understood how retail works. You get how we have to work with customers, but you also comprehend the way boutiques make profits. That's the sort of skills I need. I can teach you the rest."

"That's still a terrible way to hire someone, Juliette. For all you know, I'm actually lazy and can't be bothered to do my job when there."

She snorted at that. "Nice try, Lee. I have eyes everywhere, and you're the kind to show up to cover a co-worker's shift despite it being your day off, or a half-day, as employers do like making sure your hours bar you from benefits. I don't think the boutique will be able to strip you of benefits; they started too late, and you work too many hours. When was the last time you worked fewer than full-time hours?"

"It's been borderline thirty hours. If they cut a day a week from my schedule, my average should drop to twenty-nine. They'll have to be careful doing it because I cover too many other shifts. I won't get those shifts now, probably. I can't slide in extra hours when I'm directly told to leave. This pay might still be full-time hours—probably, unless I get screwed other days this week. I think."

"You're clever, and you've been manipulating hours in such a way it should be hard for your manager to cut your time to part-time. Also, I do not do that to my employees, as all of my employees are salaried. No matter how few hours worked, you will receive full pay, and we pay overtime despite our employees having a salary. Employees stressed about their financial situation don't work as well. I even give employees a chance to work with financial advisors to help them with their budget and money issues. I mean, there's only so much I can do, but I do try."

"What's wrong with you?" I asked.

Juliette chuckled. "Well, I am a little crazy."

"A little?"

"See? This is why you'll do just fine in my employ. You can handle the crazy. Now, get your keys out, let's go steal your stuff, and get this party started."

NINE

Why are you assuming he's sane?

NOBODY WAS HOME. I unlocked the front door and disabled the alarm as I'd been taught. Expecting Juliette to cause trouble for fun, I retrieved my harp, my framed paintings, my new collection of classic artwork prints, the Tiffany box and its precious contents, my new laptop, and a bag for the night. As expected, the woman poked around the living room, moving things around.

Clarissa's mother would not be happy when she found her bras dangling from the top of the entertainment center.

"Why are you decorating the living room with lingerie?"

"I must spread chaos where I go. I also left a ransom note. She'll find it when she gets around to taking down her favorite bras from the mantle. You've got your paintings?"

I'd been gone less than five minutes, yet I hadn't been fast enough to prevent her from creating mayhem. I sighed. "Yes, I'm bringing the paintings. I brought my prints, too. I refuse to live without them. What does the ransom note say?"

"It says I'm taking their daughter, and they can't have her

back. I left an address where they can deliver all of your things and visit you at reasonable hours."

I saw a hundred different things that could go wrong with the note. "Does the owner of the address know you have done this?"

"He will know soon enough. I thought about dropping your things off at the office, but I changed my mind. I'm going to give him a chance to counter kidnap you. But we might still go to the office first. I'll decide on the way. I'm very indecisive tonight."

"Why would any sane person wish to participate in a counter kidnapping? That I have to ask this question is disturbing."

"Why are you assuming he's sane?"

"I was hoping."

"Sanity is overrated. So are a lot of other things in life. Life is meant to be fun and happy, and that usually means abandoning society's standards for sanity. But, as I try to be a good person, you want to be the good sort of insane, not the bad sort of insane. The bad sort of insane tries to light her apartment building on fire to kill some rats."

"I have been told I shouldn't light the building on fire, but those rats deserve it. They turned my Prada into a nest. They *peed on my Prada.*"

"You'll have a new perfect black dress soon," Juliette promised, taking my laptop bag out of my hand along with my night bag. "Lock up the house and set the alarm, and we'll hit the road and make sure that you're in possession of a new black dress, a nice new home, and maybe even a new harp. There are a few great used music shops in the area, and there are pawnshops. I have time tonight. I'll troll as long as you want."

"I don't think we'll have time for all of that," I replied.

"Once you agree to become my employee, we can do this over our lunch breaks and in the evenings until we have completed our mission. I'll have to pay for all of your indulgences."

I did as ordered, making sure I locked and alarmed the house before hauling my harp to the SUV and loading it into the back. "What if I see a brand-new harp I like?"

"If I took you to a place with a brand-new harp you like, it's my foolish fault for exposing you to your dream instrument, and it's only fair I pay the price for my foolishness."

"Can we set a reasonable limit as a cap for my hiring bonus? I'm concerned you will do something even more foolish than buying a brand-new harp if left unsupervised. I'm not against a hiring bonus, but it should be a reasonable hiring bonus."

"One of my black dresses, a wardrobe suitable for working at my corporation, which I pick regardless of price but within reasonable standards, a harp, and ten thousand dollars to be spent pawnshop and thrift store shopping."

I blinked, wondering how I would be able to spend ten thousand dollars at a pawn or a thrift shop. "That sounds excessive. Ten thousand at a *thrift* store?"

"Pawnshops can have somewhat expensive purchases, especially if they're antique instruments. I figure I should be able to get you something nice at a pawnshop for that budget. It would also put you in the same general ballpark for hiring bonuses for new staff expected to work in design. If this living arrangement doesn't work out, your bonus will be adjusted to help make certain you have suitable living arrangements. I'm very hopeful this living arrangement will work out."

"Why?"

"Opposites attract."

Well, that narrowed the field down to almost every single man who had attended the Halloween party. "Rich, lives off a trust fund, possibly a player?"

"Okay, maybe not opposites attract in this case. While he's certainly comfortable, he doesn't live off a trust fund, he isn't a player, and he's actually a lot like you. Okay, similarity attracts. We'll go with that angle."

I narrowed my eyes, already regretting my decision to cooperate, and took the front passenger seat rather than retreating back to the safety of the house. "You're just making this up as you go, aren't you?"

"Oh, thank some god out there. Someone on this sweet Earth who finally understands me. In case you haven't guessed yet, we're going to be entertained because the target of my plan for your new living arrangements has no idea what's coming."

"I feel like I should somehow find a way to warn this poor man about what you're planning."

"Please don't. I'm going to blindfold you, possibly tie your hands together, and wait for his reaction. I'll record it for you since you'll be blindfolded and potentially tied up. Can you carry your harp with your hands tied together?"

A smart woman would've told the crazy woman no, but I buckled my seat belt and closed the door. Juliette dove into her SUV and locked the door. "Now, you can't escape."

"It's not a kidnapping. I got into the car willingly. This may count as stupidity, but you don't get to call it a kidnapping." I sighed and eyed the unlock button, questioning my sanity. "It counts as a kidnapping when you blindfold me and tie my hands together, but all that stuff I brought with me? I refuse to be separated from it or leave it unguarded."

"Noted. I will recruit an assistant." Juliette snatched her phone and sent a few text messages off. "The assistants will help carry everything, and I promise they won't do any damage to anything. In the worst-case scenario, I will have your harp and paintings put into the vault at work."

"This is going to be a disaster," I predicted.

"But it will be a fun disaster. I'm sure everything will work out just fine."

As it would take a miracle to convince Juliette otherwise, I remained silent.

THANKS TO TRAFFIC, it took almost two hours to reach Juliette's office building. It didn't sink in just how wealthy the woman was until she told me how proud she'd been when she'd bought the building rather than renting it floor by floor. Owning the building and its land came with its own problems, but in the long run, it was cheaper and easier than paying rent.

I struggled to come to terms with the amount of money required to buy an entire skyscraper in Manhattan. After a certain point, the numbers no longer made sense, scaled so far beyond my comprehension I couldn't imagine what it would be like to be her.

Her casual nature about my so-called hiring bonus made a lot more sense when I thought about the skyscraper.

"You bought the entire skyscraper?" I asked, aware I'd asked the same question several times before.

Juliette parked her car in the underground garage, chuckling. "If you think buying the entire building is scary, the rent was far, far worse than the mortgage on this place, not that the mortgage lasted all that long."

"Dare I ask? I'm not sure I can comprehend the value of this skyscraper."

"It didn't hurt that the previous owner was a dunce with his money and needed to unload some debt. I bought the skyscraper for ten percent over his mortgage, and as I was the only tenant in the building at the time, it made sense to him. He couldn't afford the bills and his mortgage—and I refused to allow him to skimp on the maintenance. Really, I bullied him into selling by demanding he fix what he'd been neglecting. It was getting to the point where I needed to hire my own maintenance people. The last thing he wanted was me taking him to court over it, so he sold without much of a fuss."

"I'm having a hard time believing you bullied anyone."

"I enjoy bullying land sharks. He deserved every bit of discomfort I brought to his door. If he'd honored his contracts in the first place, I wouldn't have kept badgering him about repairing things. The first time I could cite a serious safety violation due to his neglect, I won. I try to be nice, but there are limits and he was putting my employees at risk. For a while, I redirected most of my earnings into the building, and the company paid me a living wage for Hell's Kitchen. They forced it on me, really. I was going to put all my profits into making sure the building stayed in good condition. I had the plumbing replaced as I renovated everything."

Three men converged on Juliette's spot while she killed the engine and unlocked the doors. They waited for her to emerge from the vehicle before heading to the back. I hurried to claim my harp, but one of them beat me to it, and I spluttered, debating how rude it would be to take it back.

Juliette handed me the painting depicting the winter landscape, and she took the other. "Your harp will be fine. We're going to put everything in my office for the moment, then we'll strategize moving everything to your new home. First, I need to appropriately dress you, and I should have several prototypes here that should work. I'm going to dress you up before abandoning you to the wolf."

"I like how you're calling this person a wolf."

"He's a very hungry wolf."

I recognized the innuendo she attempted to foist on me before I opened my mouth. "I'm not saying what you want me to say. Also, I have a rule. No ring, no wedding plans, no nookie."

"You have a ring. It came in a blue box, and it's beautiful. I've seen pictures of the set. I believe he's badly trying to tell you he'd like you to wear that set for the wedding."

I set the painting beside me, careful to avoid damaging the frame. I lifted my hands and rubbed my temple. "That's not how this works, Juliette. First, I don't know anyone well enough to marry."

"I have decided you will enjoy a series of dates over the course of a year. They will happen nightly in the comfort of your new home. At the conclusion of the year, you will realize I'm right, be madly in love, and go through with the wedding I will plan for you. I should have gone into wedding planning instead of designing, but at least I can design for the wedding, and that's almost as good. Really, I will come up with the ideas and give bored minions extra work to do. I get bored minions near the end of a production run before the next run starts, so I have to find work for them to do, as I refuse to cut hours. I usually plan weddings. I love weddings."

"But who pays for these weddings?"

"We do not discuss that," Juliette announced, grabbing my laptop bag and settling the strap on her shoulder. "There's a fund."

I regarded her three minions, who unloaded the SUV. "Is she telling the truth?"

They grinned and nodded.

Clifford stepped around an SUV and waved at me. "It never fails to amaze me how fast Juliette works when she wants something. She didn't do anything overly aggressive this time, did she?"

"She lured me into her SUV with a chai, and being a fool, I fell for it. Next thing I knew, she was rearranging a living room with bras. I don't even know who I am anymore, Clifford. And now she's planning my wedding? I'm not even dating anyone."

"You're not dating anyone yet," he replied. "Well, kind of not dating anyone yet."

"How could I possibly be dating someone and not know it?"

"Well, the other party seems to be very bad at trying to get your attention." Clifford pointed at the painting beside me. "That, some games, a Tiffany set, and what else?"

"There is no evidence the Tiffany set is from the painting giver," I replied.

"It's from the same person," he announced.

Oh. I frowned, regarding the painting. I'd already lost an hour admiring it, wondering who had painted it, why they'd chosen a wintry waterfall as the subject, and how a piece of art could feel so cold yet so warm at the same time. "The other presents are from other people, anyway. The zombie game is from Jonas. He said he was getting it for me for Christmas."

Clifford smirked. "Was it?"

There were exactly two people who knew which games I'd enjoyed playing: Jonas and his penthouse-owning, painting-obsessed friend. The painting hadn't been in the penthouse. I'd admired every painting he'd owned. I supposed I hadn't seen a room or two, but I thought I'd seen the majority of them. Using my new phone, I texted Jonas to ask if I'd gotten the complete tour of the penthouse.

Instead of a text answer, my phone rang. Grimacing, I answered, "Hello?"

"You let Juliette into the house. Are you *mad?*"

"An absolute lunatic." Relaxing, I grinned. "I had no idea she was going to steal your mother's bras. I'm sorry. I went to get some things. I was gone five minutes, and she did all that in five minutes."

"Sounds about right. Now, why are you with Juliette?"

"Apparently, she doesn't agree with my current living arrangements and has decided I'm moving. To Manhattan."

"You don't work anywhere near Manhattan, Lee. And you refused to move in with me because I live in Manhattan."

"I tried to tell her this, but apparently, I now work in Manhattan. Who knew? Not me. I'm waiting to see papers or something like that."

"They're upstairs," Juliette announced, and she nodded in the direction of the nearby elevators. "We are going upstairs now so I can secure you as my minion."

Jonas sighed. "You fool."

"Yeah. She lured me into her vehicle with chai."

"She always finds a way to latch onto the weaknesses of

her targets. What do you want me to tell Mom and Dad? I mean, Mom's freaking because her bras are all over the house and she doesn't know why."

"There's a ransom note with the bras."

Jonas snickered. "Hey, Mom? Check for a ransom note with your bras. I believe the explanation as to why Juliette was in the house was there. Also, Shirley's fine, but she was lured into Juliette's vehicle with chai. I think Juliette may be hiring her? I overheard something about her being taken upstairs to secure her as a minion."

"I'd be sorry about this, but the chai's really good, and they cut my hours at the boutique, probably trying to bar me from insurance renewal. Then, to add insult to injury, my boss told me she's resigning next year to go to design school, so she dumped the event on me."

"I'll let my parents know."

"What are you doing at your parents' house, anyway? You live in Manhattan."

"Day off, and I always bother my parents on my days off. Didn't I tell you?"

"Tell me what?"

"I'm off for a week. Things are slow at work, so I took some time off to get a breather. Of course, I was expecting to need a week to recover from a Halloween bender, but what actually happened was a lot more fun."

"Thank you for not forcing me to put up with you while drunk."

"You're welcome. So, you're safe, and you don't need to be rescued?"

"I'm safe, and I don't need to be rescued. Juliette is excited enough about this insanity she's concocting that I'd feel bad if I ruined her fun. If she starts to bother me, I will tell her no and call for a ride to sanity. By that, I mean to *my* parents' house."

"They're here. Your parents, I mean. Mom invited them over, and they all came over at the same time, and well, your mother has now seen all of my mother's bras."

"I am so disappointed I missed that."

"Once my mother got over the shock, they started talking about bras, and at that point, Dad and I went around the house looking for you to find you'd made off with your harp and your new paintings."

"You can take my paintings out of my cold, dead hands. I don't even care if they're prints. They're mine, and you can't have them."

"What if I told you they're probably the real deal?"

"Then you definitely can't have them, they're definitely mine, and you would most certainly have to take them out of my cold, dead hands. I feel this is reasonable. They're beautiful paintings, especially the winter landscape one. That one is my favorite, and I will fight for it."

"I'll make sure everyone knows."

"I'm not going to take your paintings, and I'll make sure they're safe while we're handling matters tonight," Juliette promised.

"See, Juliette is taking care of my special needs. She knows to protect my paintings."

"When are you coming home? All four parents wish to know."

Juliette stole my phone with a maniacal laugh and said, "Which brat am I talking to? Oh. Jonas. Excellent. Tell your parents I'm keeping her forever, and they can't have her back."

I should've been more offended over her stealing my new

phone, but I couldn't wait to see what trouble the woman created next. While she dealt with Jonas, I turned to Clifford. "Is this her normal?"

"She doesn't usually take people's phones without asking first. She usually minds her manners, but I'm guessing she's excited. Which is normal when she poaches a new employee." Clifford stepped to the elevator and pressed the up button. "I really thought she'd wait at least a day before making a move. Really, Juliette?"

Juliette waved Clifford off, although she did step into the elevator when the door opened. "No. I'm not returning her. I don't care how many parents she has there wanting to see her right now. I'm at my office, and I'm employing her properly tonight. Her first assignment will be to deal with her current boutique, and I'll figure out how to get her to and from the place as needed. I'll drive her myself and work in the cafe next door if I must!"

"She really will," Clifford muttered, pressing the button for the ground floor. I squinted at the panel, which had once upon a time had other buttons that had since been removed and replaced with silvery discs.

I pointed at one of the discs. "What happened to the other floors, or is that just a weird design?"

"Juliette had this elevator converted to only go to the ground floor when she bought the building because she feels everyone should have to badge in to reach the upper levels. She has secure areas throughout the building. The other elevators have been disabled for the garage, and this one will not go to the upper floors anymore."

I found the security enhancement interesting, but I decided I'd ask about it later. Juliette laughed at something Jonas said, and I questioned everything about working for the woman and what the future might hold for me. "How does she get anything done?"

"She works every spare minute between her schemes to make up for her scheming. Some weeks, she'll disappear into her office and only emerge when her husband or son drags her out. She gets pissy if anyone other than her husband or son interrupts her while she's in a design mood. When she gets inspired to design, we might not hear from her until it's out of her system. She's causing someone trouble the rest of the time, dealing with employee issues, or generally managing the company. And she does this around the events at boutiques. Starting in two weeks, she will have daily events until mid-December."

"Daily events?" I whispered, wondering how it was possible for one woman to do so much.

"She has limited prep work she has to do; I'm on an entire team of people who help the boutiques plan the events."

"Clifford, darling?" Juliette asked, lowering my phone from her ear.

"Yes?"

"Can you take Lee to the boutique each day and cover the shore boutiques and switch with whoever is working there until she's cut loose? I've got a bunch of crybabies on the phone who will have spectacular meltdowns if I don't make arrangements."

Clifford chuckled. "We'll take care of her transportation."

"It's fine, my minions will take her to the boutique daily, and someone will bring her back. Yes, daily. No, if you steal her, you have to return her to Manhattan. This shouldn't be an issue for you. You live here."

The elevator door opened on the ground floor, and we stepped into a bright lobby with two security desks. Clifford gestured to the nearest station. "Since you don't have a badge, we have to check you—"

"The woman with the painting is with me, and if you have a problem with it, Yulan, *you're next.*"

A dark-skinned man raised his hands and crossed his fingers in a gesture of warding. "I'm happily single if you please. You can't just bring guests into the building without checking them in, Juliette."

"Yes, I can."

"No, you can't. Check her in properly."

I had no idea who Yulan was outside of being a single security guard, but I adored his ability to tell the woman no. To prevent a war from breaking out in the lobby, I strolled over, careful to avoid damaging my painting. "I'm Lee, and she's trying to hire me."

"If you need help escaping, please say so." Yulan tapped on a keyboard, and a moment later, a printer whirred. He handed over a sticker with my name on it, and it proclaimed I was Juliette's guest. "If she attempts to take you home with her, please tell her no. If possible, please tell her no where I can witness it."

"You're so mean to me, Yulan," Juliette complained. "One day, I will find the perfect woman for you, and where will you be?"

"Probably married," the guard replied with no evidence it bothered him. "But what if I want the perfect man?"

"Then I'll find the perfect man for you. Would you prefer the perfect man? I mean, if you'd like the perfect man *and* woman for you, I'm always up for a challenge, although I'm not sure how to go about that." Juliette snickered. "Hey, Jonas? What if I need to arrange for several perfect people for one of my employees? What would you suggest?"

"No," Yulan, Clifford, and everyone else in the lobby scolded.

"Why are you so mean to me?"

"I prefer one woman at a time," Yulan announced.

"Well, then why did you have to go complicating things? If you want a man, say so. If you want multiple men, say so. If you want a woman, say so. I'll accept any hints or tips on the type of perfect woman, however. You're a tough one."

"If I give you a hint, will you promise to leave me alone until next year?"

Juliette frowned, and her brows furrowed. "I'll be generous and plan to begin my campaign no sooner than February, but I've got my eye on you, Yulan."

"I don't know what I did to deserve this, but I'm very sorry." Yulan grinned and returned to his work, focusing on something on his desk.

Clifford snickered. "Looks like security just dismissed you, Juliette."

"I'm surrounded by ungrateful wretches," the woman wailed, her shoulders slumping. She sulked across the lobby to a bank of elevators. "And yes, you, too. Everyone! Except for the new one. I like her. She knows how to tell me no."

I frowned, tapping the security desk until Yulan regarded me with a raised brow. "Does she always do this when someone tells her no?"

"You'll get used to it. She's had a rough day, and this is how she vents."

"The worse her day, the more trouble she causes?"

"That sounds about right. Considering we're supposed to be in a hiring freeze, whatever your boss did must have really offended her. She usually freezes hiring and so on until January at this stage unless she finds someone really special. She's going to be yelled at by Human Resources."

"Maybe you should go up and protect her from Human Resources," I muttered.

The security guards exchanged glances.

"You know, ma'am, that's not a bad idea. Cover me," Yulan ordered, rising from his seat. "Give me a brief recap so I can keep things from getting heated."

Clifford snorted. "Typical small boutique drama. They're trying to cut her hours so they won't have to pay out insurance next year while changing her job position. Their next step will be to let her go and rehire her in a different capacity at twenty-nine hours just to be sure they don't have to pay out."

The security guards sighed, and Yulan shook his head. "One of our new launch boutiques?"

"Chosen specifically to get a closer look at Lee."

"She moved fast."

"Well, the harp had something to do with that, plus she's matchmaking again."

"I have no idea why she's matchmaking," I admitted. "And I don't see what the harp has to do with it. The Prada, that I can understand. Before the rats had trashed it, I'd really done a number on it."

"You improved the perfect dress, Lee. I saw the pictures. You took the perfect dress, and you made it better while turning it into a Halloween costume. You deserve your fate and employment opportunity." Clifford pointed at the blue box tucked under Juliette's arm. "Also, a gentleman bought you a matched set of jewelry that came in a blue box. That is not a casual gesture. And, knowing how many times Juliette has had to swoop in to rescue young men from themselves and their poor attempts at winning a lady, I have no doubt she went into panic mode. Juliette operates on anxiety half the time, and when she perceives someone she likes is having problems, she wants to make everything better. You'll get used to it."

Juliette had anxiety? My eyes widened at the thought of someone like *her* being driven by anxiety. "Anxiety? Her?"

"You should see her when she's off her medication." Yulan grunted. "Actually, don't; it's a clusterfuck. Please pardon the language. When she's off her medication, we have to call in the big guns."

"The big guns?"

"Her husband or son. They're the only people who can calm her down. Juliette's assistant takes care of the basics, including making sure she gets her breakfast, lunch, and medications on time. It doesn't help that she also has some other issues, but you'll discover those on your own."

I considered everything else I knew about Juliette, and enlightenment struck. "ADHD?"

"She's a poster child for it. She's brilliant, but she has a short attention span when she's off her meds. Add in her anxiety and work can be a roller coaster on a bad day. But on a good day?" The security guard smiled, his expression softening from affection. "That woman tries to change the world. It's not all sunny days, but she tries her best even then."

"She looks so…" I shrugged.

"With the program?" Yulan suggested.

I nodded. "That."

"Appearances can be deceiving. You'll find this company is what her dreams are made of. You'll get used to it, even on the days where everything seems like it's gone from weird to weirder. A word of advice, if I may?" Yulan walked with me to the elevator bank, where Juliette kept telling someone she had zero intentions of returning me.

"Of course."

"When she's having a bad day, treat her like every other day, even when your patience is frayed and you want to smack sense into her. Then contact her assistant and ask to have her medications checked. We're all human here, and we all make mistakes. And herding Juliette? You'd be better off handling a hundred cats. It would be easier."

I bet.

TEN

Can I stay sidelined on this one? Please? I'll beg.

THE SCREAMING match between Human Resources and Juliette started with a bang, and the Asian woman spearheading the initial assault went for Juliette's throat with a stack of papers and math. Juliette countered with a rather logical and accurate assessment of my skills, which gave her opponent enough pause for Yulan to come between the women.

"Ladies," he murmured, using his bulk to force them to take a few steps back. "Naomi, however right you are, Juliette isn't wrong to slip this one through the hiring freeze. Ask Clifford."

Clifford bowed his head. "Can I stay sidelined on this one? Please? I'll beg. I don't want to get into this tonight."

"Five minutes," Naomi ordered. "Then you can run away while I continue to teach this woman the definition of a hiring *freeze*. That does not mean hiring *spree*."

"Two is not a spree, and we *needed* that new leatherworker. *Needed.* You even agreed with me after seeing her needlework."

Naomi heaved a sigh. "I'll concede that point. Fine. Why do we *need* her?"

To spare Clifford from participation, I announced, "I improved the perfect Prada. But then rats invaded my apartment and peed on it. And since peeing on it wasn't bad enough, they shredded it and turned it into a nest."

Naomi's mouth dropped open, then she snapped her teeth together with a wince-worthy clack. She turned to Juliette and pointed at me without a word.

Juliette shrugged and held her hands up in a helpless gesture. "I got on my knees and hugged her legs at the costume party. I cried, Naomi. She even had little felt bats on the dress, and a beautiful crystal belt. I don't know what happened to that belt, but if it can't be saved, I am paying her to make another one. It was brilliant, and I think we could build an entire New Age line around it."

"New Age and modern fashion don't mix, Juliette," Clifford muttered. "And we're not rigged for full vegan sourcing yet. We've talked about this."

"We can establish a vegan-friendly line. I'll just have to open a branch and build it from the ground up. And it's not like people won't pay high amounts for ethically sourced vegan goods. It will just raise the bottom line. We can do it during a strong year and buffer the initial losses that way."

Once again, everyone sighed.

I set my painting on my feet so the frame wouldn't be damaged by the floor. "If you're going vegan, you may as well go all American, too. You're already dealing with an expensive line, and if you appeal to patriotic pride, you create more jobs, you appeal to a new audience, and you focus on being ecologically responsible. I mean, don't your clothes already cost a fortune? Are people who want to buy your clothes and buy into these lines already willing to pay high costs for it? Just add the differences in manufacturing to the bill. If you can work with local suppliers, then you have even better options, don't you? It just means you need more people like Clifford, and that raises your bottom line."

"And you wondered why I want her," Juliette said, taking her turn pointing at me. "Do you have any idea how rare common sense is?"

Naomi planted her hands on her hips. "As I deal with you daily, I'm very aware of how rare common sense is."

Wow. "Most places I've worked, that would be a firing offense."

"You'll get used to it," everyone announced.

Would I? I had my doubts, but I decided it didn't matter. I'd do as I always did until I got a better feel for what, exactly, I'd get used to.

Juliette patted my arm. "We have lines of professionalism, but I value honesty more than professionalism. Now, that said, we do not tolerate prejudices. We have clients of all shapes, sizes, and nationalities, and we do not engage in prejudiced behavior. Sure, I lose some clients because I welcome everybody, but I don't want those clients anyway. They can keep their money. There are plenty of better people who will pay my price tags—and I have lines in the works for people on a budget. I'm hoping I can make use of local suppliers to create locally inspired lines. That'll be a challenge, though, as I'll have to spend a week in every area we do this in at a minimum."

"That sounds amazing," I admitted.

"Naomi?"

"I don't want to know."

"But you're going to find out anyway."

"You're going to tell me I'm releasing the hiring freeze for this as an exception, and I'm not going to like what you tell me, but I'm going to do it anyway, because you're going to concoct the required fifty reasons to go outside of the hiring freeze, so let's get to it. You have five minutes. Convince me."

"She would have to present a reason every six seconds to present fifty reasons to hire me. Is that even possible?" I realized I cut into Juliette's precious seconds. "Sorry."

"That counts as five reasons," Juliette announced. "Pause time a moment, please."

"I hadn't started my timer, so it's okay, and I'll consent to the reason count."

I tried to figure out how my question could possibly count as five reasons. "I don't think that's how math works."

With a giggle, Juliette rubbed her hands together. "Fifty reasons is how Human Resources makes me justify a hiring. A reason can be a lot of things. So, what you said has a lot of reasons to make you a good hire. First, you demonstrated basic common sense. That's worth two points because we value common sense highly. All demonstrations of common sense are worth two points. Correct math skills are worth a point, but you get an extra point for being able to do it as quickly as you did without a calculator. You also got a point for demonstrating a realization you may have overstepped and immediately addressed the situation. Technically, I should have asked for six points, as you demonstrated empathy for someone else."

"I'll consent to six points," Naomi replied. "That still leaves you with forty-four reasons."

"Well, Lee? Game for seeing how many points you can

collect for yourself in five minutes? Treat it like an introductory interview, one where you're asked to present as much information about yourself as you can. Don't be shy. If you think that it's useful for our type of business, go ahead and say it."

"You're evil, Juliette. I should tell you no just so you have practice at accepting that as an answer."

Naomi laughed. "I should consent to hiring you just for that. We usually have to train people to push back against Juliette. No wonder she likes you. All right. I'm not going to make you stick to the five minutes, as that's a restriction she needs, else she would take an hour trying to concoct reasons I should hire you. Let's call it fifteen minutes."

"Honestly, I have no idea why Juliette wants to hire me this badly. I adjusted my Prada because it was the only black dress I had. I saved up for years to earn that dress, but my friend had invited me somewhere, and I didn't want to hurt her feelings or embarrass her, so I destroyed my dress."

"She improved a perfect Prada, Naomi. That's the only reason I need."

"The rules are the rules, Juliette. Fifty reasons or you'd try to hire everyone in the entire state. Our profits are good, but they're not that good, especially since you refuse to hoard money in a bank account. And don't you complain to me. You're the one who made the rules. And I'd like to remind you why we're under a hiring freeze."

"We're under a hiring freeze because we don't have a full five years of employee salaries and company operations in our bank account, and we shouldn't hire new employees unless we can guarantee we can keep everyone for five years. This is my rule, and I should abide by it. But she's perfect," Juliette whined.

"Your opinion of her perfection is worth a single point and only a single point."

Juliette pouted.

I could live for fifteen minutes of trying to come up with reasons I was worth the company's attention. Most job interviews were at least that long. It was just an interview with a weird approach to how people were hired. I lifted my chin. "I don't have a college degree because my family was too poor for me to go. Even if I had gotten financial aid, we couldn't afford the student loan bill afterward, so I didn't bother going to college. I entered the workforce right out of high school. I have done some customer service work, but I ultimately went into retail, and I've been working retail ever since. I'm not stupid, but I'm not educated, either."

Naomi and Juliette exchanged looks, but neither spoke. The rest of her employees shuffled their weight, and I wondered what they expected from employees and degrees.

Most companies wanted someone who could finish college.

"I'm good at budgeting because I have no choice but to be good at budgeting. Most weeks, I'm lucky if I have twenty dollars here and there. Honestly, I have no idea what's going to happen at this point; I lost hours at the boutique, and I'm used to taking care of myself because there's no one who can afford to take care of me. My parents can't afford much, especially not a freeloader, so I can't freeload. So, if you need someone who has already got a heavy dose of reality, I'm your woman. The only reason I'm going along with Juliette's scheme is because I was told that I'd be paid a living wage. I'm not paid a living wage right now, but I have to make a living wage because I have no choice."

"I would like to say that thanks to the rat infestation of

her apartment, she has been coerced into accepting an invitation with her second parents, so she is not nearly that bad off, but I expect she's going to fight them over the rent. I've come up with a better alternative." Juliette pointed at me. "And no protesting out of you. You will fight tooth and nail to pay your fair share of the rent, and I won't let your stubborn pride come in the way of you and your perfect man."

"I'm not sure that's how dating, love, and relationships work, Juliette."

"It is when I'm involved."

"You are a menace, but you're too friendly. Stop being a friendly menace. It's hard to tell friendly menaces no, but if you do something stupid, or this mystery man isn't comfortable, I will tell you no."

"This mystery man adores everything about you, but he's an awkward little coward and has no idea how to approach you outside of making it look like he's a stalker. Society has taught him men should show interest by buying things, and you're not the kind who wants a man buying things for you."

"Are you a psychologist as well as a fashion designer?"

"It's a part of being a designer. I have to match the person with their clothes. I can't make clothes that sing to a client if I don't understand how my client thinks. Clothing is an expression of self."

"So, you should just tell him to see me, have him tell me he's interested, and we'll see what happens from there. But I will have questions."

"If I throw you in headfirst, you'll swim. If I let you dip your toes in, you'll have a wet toe and nothing else to show for it," Juliette predicted. "My way will get the job done, and nothing lets two people get to know each other better than sharing the same roof. You'll figure out if you have chemistry immediately, and you're both the type to make it work if you have sufficient motivation. Living together will provide that motivation. I will not say what I think will be happening within a week, as there's a pair of virgin ears in the room."

Yulan heaved a sigh. "I'm single, Juliette. That doesn't mean I'm a virgin."

"You're a virgin. I pranced a model in lingerie through the lobby and almost gave you a heart attack. I can't prance models through the lobby when you're on shift, as I don't want to lose a good employee due to panty exposure."

"This is one of those situations where you tell her no and send her to her room to think about what she's done, Yulan. Also, it doesn't matter if you're a virgin or not, and it's none of her business, either." I pointed at Juliette. "No. Leave him alone and behave yourself."

"I haven't even gotten to sign your hiring agreement yet, and you're already assertive."

"He's like a gentleman-in-distress, and if you're not controlled, you're going to prance women in panties around him until he's numb to their presence, then you'll try to marry him to one of the models."

Juliette's eyes widened. "I hadn't thought of matchmaking one of the models. That's a really good idea."

"Unless Yulan asks you to parade interested women in panties out in front of him, the answer is no. You do not marry people to each other because she looks pretty in panties, and he likes a pretty woman in panties."

"All women are pretty in panties," Juliette replied.

"While that may be the case, Yulan might be an intellectual with an appreciation for women in pretty panties. Anyway, unless he specifically asks you to matchmake for him, the answer is no."

"But what if I meet the woman perfect for him?"

"Tell her of his location, return to work, and don't indulge in any unnecessary—" I narrowed my eyes. "No, I misspoke. Do not indulge in any kidnappings. Period."

"That did not take you long to figure out. I'm so proud of you. See, Naomi? That has to be worth fifty points alone. That said, you allowed me to kidnap you."

"You lured me into your SUV with a chai, and I consented to be driven to Manhattan, as I recognized you would not be happy until you had a chance. As this could result in the first time I might have a job where I don't have to work miracles with my budget, I thought it was worth the risk."

"You could sell the Tiffany jewelry and be set for a while. I figure you could get a hundred thou for it without much trouble. I don't think you will, but that's okay. You could. And the painting with the flowers is easily worth a cool half a million if you didn't mind selling to a museum. Maybe more. I'd have to check into the artist. While no Monet, that one's still worth a pretty penny."

My throat dried, and my heart rate skyrocketed. "I've been carting around a painting worth how much?"

"Me and my big mouth. See, that's the problem with you two! He bought what he thought you would like, and he didn't even think twice about the price. He thought you would like it, and that's that. You know the value of money, and now you're going to try to figure out how to give it back because it's too valuable because you don't think someone like you should have something so precious. But he's right, and he has already decided your value, which is very high to him." Juliette stomped her foot. "Hire her so I can marry them, Naomi! Also, I don't know the value of your favorite painting. I've never seen that one before."

"I want to say this is not how this works, but when you get involved, this is exactly how it works." Shaking her head, Naomi flung her hands in the air along with the folder of papers, which scattered. "Fine."

Juliette nudged one of the sheets of paper with her toe. "I'm pretty sure you just threw a copy of the employee handbook on the floor. Possibly our standard insurance policy, and maybe a copy of the employee hiring questionnaire?"

"Accounting is going to come to my office tomorrow, and I'm going to get paddled."

My eyes widened. "Paddled?"

Naomi nodded. "Accounting will tell my husband I couldn't tell Juliette no again, and he'll whack me with one of the production rejects, probably a boot. As I'll deserve it for not telling her no, I'll just yell at Juliette over the extra paperwork going through Human Resources."

"Well, as long as you like it, I guess that's okay." I would regret that later. Juliette would recognize my weaknesses and exploit them.

The women both leered at me.

"That is shameless and disgusting."

Rather than being offended, they laughed.

"He won't paddle her. He'll just be smug and threaten her with it, and then for some reason, they always leave work early." Juliette shrugged. "It's such a strange coincidence they always leave early on the days Naomi fails to tell me no."

I wondered why. Rolling my eyes, I picked up my painting, regarding the wintry scene. "The other painting is really worth that much? Do you think this one is, too? There were a bunch of prints in the case, too. They could be prints, right?"

"They're real. That's what you'd like, so that's what he got. It's a rare thing when people do their best to make someone else happy. The obvious solution is to make you live with him and see how well you get along. He's a gentleman, and I expect you to be a lady. As such, you'll have to behave your-self, even if he prances around half-naked in his home. And he'll have to behave if you prance around half-naked."

She had to be talking about the Penthouse Guy. I still didn't know his name, and he'd already figured me out from top to bottom. No one else made sense.

I couldn't even blame the guy; women who valued art as much as I did came few and far between, and if he decided to talk about any one of his pieces, he'd have a captive audience who'd never get bored of him or his art.

Damn. I should've just asked Jonas to pitch that as an offer rather than wait around and hope he'd invite me over for coffee.

"That's not how that works," Naomi muttered.

"Well, he doesn't get to admire her in pretty panties until he's agreed to marry her and set a date. That's her rule, not mine. I mean, I'd totally suggest she take him for a test drive if it were my business, but it's not."

"I see Clarissa has been notifying the world of my personal preferences."

"She can't tell me no. You should give her some lessons. She could use them."

"I'm not paid enough to deal with this."

"Yet," Juliette corrected. "You're not paid enough to deal with this yet. Go to Naomi's office. She'll get you settled. And don't you worry about this mess on the floor. I'll clean it up, as I know she has at least ten copies of this blank file at all times. I'm really good at finding fifty reasons someone should be hired, though to be fair to me, you earned all your points on your own."

I had? "Will my paintings and the blue box be safe in your office?"

"No, but they'll be safe in the vault, and I'll have everything locked away until you're ready to leave or someone takes them over to your new home. Yulan? Want to get someone to open it up and register everything, so it's safe? I promised her some pawnshop time, too. So, call it four hours until we need to pick it up. Ask around if someone would like some overtime to let us in after. I'll call if there's an issue or she's being claimed and won't be able to fetch everything tonight."

I handed my precious painting to Yulan. "Thank you, and I'm sorry for the extra work."

"Don't worry. I'll have fun with her in a week or two. Every now and then, she needs a reminder that security handles her badge, and it's fun making her come to the desk to reactivate hers. But we're nice and do it on days the delay won't scandalize her much."

"I think you just miss me, so you lure me to the front desk."

"That is exactly it, Juliette. We miss you because you only visit us when you want to bring a guest into the building," Yulan replied with a smirk.

"Fine. You win. You want pizza again, don't you?"

"How did you guess we like pizza?"

"Because for some reason, you cretins guilt me into feeding you pizza at least twice a month. I'll amuse myself and order you bottomless pits some pizza while Naomi takes care of Lee."

I took that as my cue to escape while I could, and I went with Naomi to find out just how crazy Juliette actually was.

I LEARNED a few eye-opening facts about life in New York City. According to the various living-wage calculators, assuming I shared an apartment with someone, I could survive somewhat comfortably in the area for a mere forty thousand a year. Naomi grinned while I went over the estimated living expenses, speculating how I could make it work on that budget.

"Lee."

I looked up from the printed sheets she'd given me to review about general frugal life in New York City. "What?"

"You don't have to make your life work on that budget. There's exactly no one in this company who makes that little."

I frowned, regarding the papers again. "But this is the living wage, isn't it?"

Naomi pointed at the rental column. "That's assuming you have a roommate to help cover the rent for a decent apartment. We calculate our living wage by a single person living alone in one of those apartments, and then we make certain that your rent is no higher than twenty percent of your pay—after taxes. The company covers the entirety of your health insurance, so that will not be a factor."

I sucked in a breath. "How does the company even afford to hire so many people when that's the base pay?"

"The black dress I was informed would be yours typically

costs fifteen thousand dollars, but she picked one from an unreleased line. We have a lot of those; we will release additional lines at slightly lower costs if we are having a slim month. Juliette's currently working out how to make a line of quality clothing we can sell for an affordable amount—for people like you, not for the rich and famous who want to walk down the red carpet in a custom Carter. Juliette designs those, too. Those are substantially more expensive."

"How expensive? Do I want to know?"

"A minimum of a hundred thousand for the design work, then there's material, employee expenses, and sales taxes. Juliette also has very specific rules on the type of changes a client may request for a custom outfit. If she's expected to design jewelry or accessories, she also charges another design fee. If the design can't be used again and is a true exclusive, the design fee is doubled, and she signs a contract that bars that specific design from being used again. If the design may be used again, it's exclusive to the client for a period of three years, and then it undergoes minor alterations. Most don't go exclusive, so Juliette will get to reap the benefits of the dress or suit down the road. Those tend to sell really well, too. It's usually her best work."

"It sounds complicated."

"It is. So, I have you flagged for potential design alterations and boutique management."

"Like Clifford does?"

"Not quite; you'd be potentially recruited to manage our actual boutique. It's invitation-only, and you would work with clients to get a feel for what they need from Juliette. Then Juliette will work with them directly once they've been given the introduction. Juliette can be overbearing with the clients, so we try to prepare them for working with her. It's a part of the experience. And this part is important: If they like you, and they like your design work, you'll work with Juliette to create their wardrobe."

"Wait. Create their wardrobe? From scratch?"

"We have clients who want unique clothes, and they're willing to pay for it. Some of our clients are known to cut a check for several million and ask for new clothes. Juliette will do this for less than her typical custom work if they agree to only six months of exclusivity. Part of your job will be figuring out what the client needs and sifting through the hundreds of test designs Juliette has made to match the outfits with the client. You'll be challenged. It's a good job, and it pays well." Naomi's eyes widened, and she grinned. "I have an idea."

"I have never been so afraid of four words in my entire life."

"That's because you're smart. I just had a beautiful way to test drive your skills and give Juliette what she wants." The woman grabbed the phone and stabbed at the buttons. "Juliette, you should invite Lee's gentleman for a fitting and tell him you'll do his wardrobe, but he has to work with Lee. If they can survive that, they'll survive anything."

I could clearly hear Juliette's cackle on the other end of the line.

"Take over suits and make him try them on for her. You'll test their chemistry. Bring over some lingerie in her size and watch them both question their boundaries. It'll be fun."

It would? I foresaw disaster and temptation.

The eligible pool of people crazy enough to buy me anything, especially a painting and prints matching what I liked, consisted of one person. He'd already proven he could tempt me with his mouth and been a shining example of patience even when he'd discovered me in his penthouse with his friend playing games on his entertainment system.

He'd been at the park, too.

That left him with a very small window of opportunity to acquire everything, and he would've had to do it around his busy life, a life Jonas had implied meant everything to him. Maybe many wouldn't care, but if it was him, he'd tried to make space in his life for me without me being aware of it.

People gambled all the time. Sometimes, they lost. Sometimes, they won. Sometimes, they broke even.

But nobody could win without tossing the dice.

"All right. I'll do that." Naomi hung up. "She's all in, and she's hunting for suits that will fit him. She's going to dress you in a black dress and pretty panties, and she'd appreciate if you didn't put up a fuss over it."

I wouldn't know if I'd win or lose unless I gambled, and there were worse ways to live life. I couldn't build something from nothing, but I could take a risk, gamble, and try. And if I did lose, I wouldn't live the rest of my life wondering what might have happened if I'd only been brave enough to try. "If she's going to put me in a black dress, then I'm going to need my blue box."

Naomi smiled. "Now we're talking business. Let's get your paperwork all sorted so you can get on with the rest of your night."

ELEVEN

This is the only part of my plan that survived.

MY NEW SALARY stunned me into cooperating with Juliette and her gang of minions.

I doubted anyone had a concrete plan for the evening. Instead of a trip to explore nearby pawnshops, Juliette tested black dress after black dress on me until she declared a floor-length gown with a slit up to my thigh as the winner. When she gave me the choice of heels, boots, or sandals, I picked the sandals as the candidate least likely to murder my feet within five minutes.

One call summoned a young woman armed with a comb and a bag filled with accessories meant to transform me from a magpie into a black swan. It took her an hour, but she transformed my hair into blooming roses fashioned into a crown, similar to how Jonas had styled my hair for the trip to the park. Juliette declared I didn't need any makeup, handed me a black purse with red accents that matched my jewelry, and herded me to the lobby.

The only piece of Tiffany jewelry I didn't wear was the

ring, as it was a little too large. Afraid I'd lose it, it went back into the box, which was locked in Juliette's office safe so she could retrieve it for resizing later.

Then she presented a pair of black, fuzzy handcuffs and a blindfold. "So far, this is the only part of my plan that survived."

"I feel my harp and paintings should be going with us."

"I'll have them delivered after you're settled. You don't need to seduce him with your harp. You just have to show up."

"You're assuming there will be a seduction."

"You look like a billion dollars, and you're wearing sensible shoes. He may be shy, awkward, and clueless, but honestly, you don't have to be wearing anything to success-fully seduce him."

"Seductions tend to require the removal of clothing," I reminded her.

"I said that wrong. You don't have to be wearing anything special to seduce him. You could be in your pajamas and seduce him. You could wear teddy bear footsies and seduce him without having to do more than order him to bed. I have observed him. Of course, you'll have to crack his shell a bit to get him to talk, but I think you'll have plenty of common ground to work on. Now, hands in front of you. I have cuffs to apply."

"I refuse to be cuffed until we're close to our destination, but I'll deal with the humiliation of the blindfold if you feel it's really necessary."

"It's not necessary, but it would make me happy. It would also let me see his reaction. It should be spectacular. Want me to record it?"

"No."

"But—"

"No."

Our audience laughed, and Yulan returned to his work. "Enjoy your evening, Lee."

"You're next," I swore.

"Alas, I am not. I have until February before I must worry about her scheming. There are two full months of opportunities for Juliette to poke her nose in someone else's business. She'll start searching for people to put together after two weeks. I'm safe."

"For now."

"You're going to fit right in here. Go have a good time and try not to let Juliette do something you'll regret later," he advised.

"Give me the damned blindfold. If I'm going to do this, I'll do it to myself, at least that way I can accept I'm the one who did this to me."

Juliette complied and grinned. "You're such a good sport."

"I'm an idiot, but I'm unfortunately curious about what kind of man would be interested in having *you* try to marry him off to *me*."

"A smart, wise one. Don't tell my husband this, but he's rather handsome, and I'm really looking forward to treating him like a doll. And he'll let me do it, because I know these suits will fit, and I'll leave him a discounted—"

"No," everyone in the lobby announced.

"I feel like I've missed something," I muttered, debating if I wanted to wait before putting on the blindfold or getting it over with and accepting my fate. Instead of telling her no and leaving, I slipped the fabric over my eyes and tied it into place.

Clifford chuckled and patted my arm. "She is too fond of

trying to give discounts, and we have to tell her no. We have limited conditions we'll let her cut losses, and it usually involves hiring her target as a model, giving away the clothes as part of a hiring bonus, or making some other monetary arrangement worth a similar amount. Someone will coach you on your first full day here."

"That'll happen after the launch at her boutique. Lee, you do not need to notify your employer you have been hired by me, by the way."

"Isn't that a conflict of interests?"

"No. You're working in their interest to make sure the boutique has a successful launch, and you're allowed to accept employment whenever you want. If they wanted to keep you, they wouldn't have cut any hours. I bet you they'll cut more hours on you tomorrow."

"I have no idea how I'm getting to work tomorrow."

"I already said I'll take you," Clifford replied with a chuckle. "I need to go to the boutique anyway, so I'll just go when you need to be there. It'll work out. As I know exactly where she's taking you, it's not far from here, so it won't be out of the way to pick you up. I have to come here for paper-work before I go to the boutique anyway."

"It's really not an inconvenience?"

"It's really not."

"Okay. What should I do with Juliette if she gets out of hand?"

"Give her something shiny. She'll amuse herself."

I laughed. "She wouldn't do that." Hesitating, I turned in Clifford's direction despite my inability to see him. "Would she?"

"I totally would," Juliette replied. "There's a vehicle out

front, so get the suits loaded before she changes her mind while I handle her."

"I'm not going to change my mind. Just be careful. The last thing I need is to break my ankle tonight." Or get stung by a bee. Or abandon my common sense altogether while falling prey to Juliette's scheming. "I have a list of things I don't need tonight. Snapping my ankle is fairly high up on the list."

"What else is on your list?" Juliette took my arm. Clifford gave me a departing pat on the shoulder before wishing me a good night as he left.

"Not being stung by a bee."

"Those are mostly done for the year, so you have little to fear. I haven't seen a bee in weeks, not that they're common around here anyway."

"The keyword there is mostly."

"What else?" With a gentle touch, she led me across the lobby, guided me through the front doors, and herded me into a waiting vehicle. "I mean, I get your reasoning for having bees on your list. Who wants to be stung by a bee?"

"I have developed an aversion to rats. Human or rodent varieties. No more rats."

"That's reasonable. I promise you I would never arrange a wedding for a rat of any variety."

As I'd already lost my mind agreeing to go anywhere with Juliette while blindfolded, I said, "I bet you could make a really cute wedding dress for a rat."

"I draw the line at designing clothing for mice and rats. No. Over my dead body. I will dress up cats and dogs, but I will not dress up a rat, not after what they did to your Prada. I've declared war on them for that."

"You're something else, Juliette."

"That I am, but admit it, Lee. You like me."

"It disturbs me that I do."

"It's because you're one of the more sensible people I've hired. Don't tell Naomi this, but that was worth fifty points right there, though she'll never admit it. What else is on your list?"

"Discovering this was all some dream, and in reality, I died overworking myself or something stupid like that."

"I try not to overwork my employees, and I never require overtime. I will ask if anyone is interested in overtime, but now that I know you're one of those, I will take steps."

"Those?"

"Workaholics."

"This is a pot calling kettle black situation, Juliette."

"My husband keeps telling me that for some reason."

"I'll cut you a deal. If you don't tell anyone I work hard to make ends meet, I won't tell anyone you work hard to make ends meet. You're just a lot better at it than I am."

"I think you're doing pretty well, actually. You'll be plenty comfortable with your new salary, and I think you'll love your new living arrangements almost as much as the man who currently resides there."

"Has anyone told you that you're prone to laying it on thick?"

"At least five times a day. Why?"

"They're probably right."

Juliette laughed. "Oh, I know they're right. I just don't care."

AS PROMISED, the drive wasn't far to our next destination, and while the street was New York noisy, the inside of the building was eerily quiet. Juliette shushing everyone had something to do with that, and I marveled that the witnesses actually cooperated with her. She recruited several people in the lobby to help cart her collection of suits upstairs.

It only took her a few snaps of her finger, a please, and a thank you to gain some helpers. I believe they wanted to witness her insanity.

A blindfolded woman decked out in a fortune of clothing and jewels didn't come around every day, and New Yorkers loved free entertainment.

Riding in an elevator blindfolded disconcerted me, especially with the damned thing stopping at several floors before we reached our destination. Juliette guided me with a hand on my elbow, and after a somewhat long walk, she knocked on a door. "Open up, you! I brought a present."

The door creaked, and I blurted, "You should grease that."

Juliette laughed. "Wow, Lee. You went straight for the throat."

"No, I went straight for the hinges. They squeak. It'll take a little oil and five minutes to fix if that. I can do it tonight."

"Not in that dress, you aren't!"

"I'd change first."

"Into what, exactly?"

Realization dawned that the tricky woman had stolen my clothes. "You are a terrible human being, Juliette Carter!"

"Revenge is sweet, isn't it? It's also best served in a sexy dress."

"You are a terrible, horrible human being. Evil, too. Wretched. You did that on purpose. You stole my clothes, and you made your innocent employees distract me while you did it."

"Your new dress is so much better if I do say so myself."

"Why have you brought insanity to my door, Juliette?"

Well, shit. Juliette's general belief about the situation made a great deal more sense knowing she'd dragged me to the Penthouse Guy's home. Running might work, but Juliette knew where my parents, second parents, and friends all lived, which left me with few viable escape routes. "This is Jonas's fault, isn't it?"

"No, it's your fault. You had an entire hallway of candidates to choose from, and you went for him. You made the bed, so I recommend you start sleeping in it," Juliette replied, her tone smug. "I brought suits, and they should fit you without alteration, but if you want the suits, you have to agree to allow this woman to live with you. Rats invaded her apartment, and she was forcefully ejected from her residence. Dragged out, really, from what I've been told. I wasn't there, but Jonas was."

"I've already heard about the rats and the dress. I see you found an even better one for her. I like it"

"Found? What do you mean by that, you cretin? Found? Found?" Juliette's voice rose an octave. "I didn't find that dress. I made it!"

The Penthouse Guy chuckled, and his victory over the woman went into the pro column of living in the sort of penthouse I dreamed about. "Why did you blindfold Lee?"

"I felt like it."

As I'd already reached the point of no return, I'd do my best to enjoy myself. I removed the blindfold, and an amused, shirtless Penthouse Guy kept a close eye on a fuming Juliette. Somehow, I'd stumbled my way directly into heaven, and I didn't care he lacked the defined abs most women liked. Fit without being muscle bound was more my speed. He checked off every box and scored bonus points in the process. "I've figured out most of what she does is for that reason. It was easier to go with the insanity than protest it, and she lured me into her car with chai." I shrugged, aware I confessed to being an idiot, although I thought I'd done well keeping from blurting the rest of my thoughts out. "I think this is her revenge for altering my Prada."

"Damn straight, it's revenge for adjusting an already perfect dress. You're supposed to improve the ones that aren't already perfect. You're only allowed to do that to my dresses from now on."

"I apologize for her, Lee. She gets out of control whenever she's left unsupervised. You don't have to do anything she says unless you want to."

"Well, I foolishly agreed to be her employee, so I have to do some of the things she tells me."

"That's fast, even for you, Juliette. Also, I feel like I've failed to protect her from you."

"Her boutique cut her hours, and Clifford kept telling me things I didn't like. I decided to fix the situation. I was performing a rescue mission. But, yes. You failed. Your penance is to tuck her into your bed tonight."

"Or the guest bedroom, as I won't take advantage of a lady when you're masterminding something. What that something is, I'm not really sure, but I've made a few educated guesses."

"Your wedding."

Well, Juliette was honest and forthcoming. I could respect that. More importantly, I could handle life in a penthouse with a man who countered with the existence of a guest bedroom while Juliette did her best to get me to sleep with him. All while in front of her well-dressed group of volunteers, a few of whom I recognized from the party. Rather than ditching my own rules and suggesting I'd be interested, especially if he insisted on walking around his own home shirtless, I kept my mouth shut.

"Well, as I see you're on a mission, and I know you well enough to know I may as well hear what you have in mind, come on in. I'm not even sure you how got my neighbors to help you, but it probably involves blackmail and coercion."

Everyone laughed, even me. "She just asked nicely. They're New Yorkers, and there was free entertainment available. Did you expect anything different?"

"Not particularly. Thank you for taking your blindfold off, as I'd rather not have to rescue you or one of my paintings from a Juliette-created accident. Unless you want to be rescued, in which case, do as you please."

Juliette would, and because she would, I threw the blindfold at the fashion designer. "You're a terrible person."

"I really am. It's wonderful. But he offered to rescue you if you wanted. That's a good start, right?"

"I would apologize for her, except she's really not sorry, nor will she ever be sorry." I straightened my shoulders and took the first step into his penthouse, and my gaze locked onto the sketch proudly displayed on his wall. "I still owe you a coffee."

"If Juliette gets her way, it seems we can have coffee or tea every morning, although I must admit, I was not expecting to have company today."

I expected he would've put on a shirt if he'd been expecting company, although I appreciated the view. "I'm blaming the rats, Jonas, and Juliette. The rats get more of the blame, but I've been told I'm not allowed to light my apartment on fire. Ex-apartment. We've suffered a breakup. A rat peed on my harmonica."

"Please tell me your harp is safe."

I smiled at his concern for my instrument.

"It's in the vault at my work," Juliette said, strolling across the entry to admire the artwork. "So are her new paintings and prints. She's pretty jealous over the paintings, which she assumed are prints. I told her they aren't."

"While I did get prints knowing she liked classical art, the paintings are the real deal. The flowers I had gotten a few weeks ago, but I hadn't figured out where to hang it. Then I figured you'd appreciate it more, Lee."

"And the winter painting?"

"That's a secret."

I liked secrets, especially when they were presented with an invitational tone challenging me to find out all about it. "No matter what Juliette says, I can't afford the rent on this place even if I wanted to, but I'm willing to overlook my shortcomings to be able to admire your paintings whenever I want."

He laughed. "You have no idea what my name is, do you?"

"Not a clue in hell."

"Christopher."

"I'm assuming you know my name, as you managed to get the paintings mailed without incident."

"I can be convincing when necessary."

I had no idea what everyone thought was so funny about his comment, but his neighbors burst into laughter, and Juliette snickered, shook her head, and began the process of reclaiming suits from her volunteers. "I can be convincing, too. You have to try on all of these suits so I can have them adjusted as needed. The rest of you, out! Thank you, but you're not getting sneak peeks at him until he's clothed to my satisfaction."

I regarded Christopher's bare chest with a raised brow.

"Any more of a sneak peek than you've already gotten," the designer muttered. "Why are you half-naked, Chris?"

"This is my house, and at this hour, if I want to be half-naked in my house, I can be. It's your fault for showing up unexpectedly. If you wanted me dressed, you should've called ahead."

I considered his words carefully. "So, if we want to see you naked, all we have to do is show up unexpectedly?"

Juliette covered my mouth with her hand. "Unless you want to see him naked, don't give him ideas."

Damn it. Why had I promised myself I needed a wedding date, ring, and plans for the future? I sighed.

"I've gotten the lecture, Juliette. No ring, no wedding date, and no future plans means all she gets to see is my chest when she wanders in unexpectedly. I'm not responsible if she comes into the bathroom while I'm using it, however. I do usually close the door."

Keyword: usually.

"I'm game to plan your wedding for Halloween next year. If I'm busy planning your wedding, I won't be able to interrupt your evening dates. For the record, she enjoys chai sprinkled with cinnamon and nutmeg, and you'll have a very attentive audience should you be in a mood to discuss art. Also, I couldn't help but notice you'd included an engagement band in the box you'd acquired. It's a half size too large, but that's easily fixed, especially since it's locked in my safe at work. I can take care of it."

"That's not how this works," I reminded Juliette.

"It really is when I'm involved. I can't help it if people recognize when I'm talking good sense. Sure, it's a little spontaneous, but it's still good sense."

"A little?"

"I'm confident enough to be willing to put in the work planning a Halloween wedding. If the shoe fits, I say you should wear it. The shoe definitely fits. You two will be too busy admiring art and going to galleries to fight."

"I don't know what reality you live in, but I'm torn between asking for a ride to it or running away," I admitted.

"If you run away, she'll chase you," Christopher warned me. "That's what she does. And then she'll recruit others to help chase you. Anyway, you're more than welcome to make use of my guest bedroom, especially as you fell into Juliette's clutches. It's a short enough of a walk to her office, but if you need a ride in the morning, I drive by it on my way to work."

"Where do you work?"

"Close enough that I can walk, but I usually have to drive because of business meetings. I can show you the building over the weekend."

Juliette resumed herding everyone out of Christopher's penthouse, neatly sorting the suits on the floor. Once she'd gotten rid of her volunteers, she gestured to the sea of black bags. "The sooner you consent to be my doll, the sooner I leave, Chris. Then you can do whatever it is you do with your evenings when you have an unexpected and permanent house guest."

"Well, I was originally going to shower, but my showering plans were interrupted. I find the interruption to be well worth it, however. That said, did you really confiscate her clothing?"

"I really did."

"She needs clothes, Juliette."

"I figured she'd wear one of your shirts until I send Clifford over in the morning with work-appropriate attire."

Christopher shook his head and sighed. "Do you ever sleep?"

"I'm goading my husband into retrieving me tonight."

"I feel someone should warn him."

"He already knows. I pitched a hissy fit earlier today, demanding attention. He told me I'd get my attention after a late meeting tonight."

"And that was a reason to kidnap Lee?"

"I have a list of reasons a mile long why I needed to kidnap Lee. Hiring her was at the top. You came in at a close third."

"Dare I ask what came in second?"

As I wanted to know, too, I kept my mouth shut and listened.

"Dressing her up for my enjoyment. I've never tried my hand at period gowns before, but after seeing her in one at the park, I'm determined to make a few. I'll have her model them for me."

I opened my mouth to reject her offer, thought twice about it, and snapped my teeth together. At a complete loss for what to do, I stared at Christopher.

"Just go with it, Lee. Juliette loves pretty things, and you were very pretty in your gown."

"Well, it wasn't mine. Jonas borrowed it. I wish I could afford the slippers that went with it, though."

"You can. The slippers were my contribution. They're normally made for indoor use at home for those who don't like to go barefoot. They're the cheapest product I make, and honestly, they're usually just made for employees to wear around the office to make sure they're comfortable. The seamstresses and tailors love them. They cost me about five dollars a pair to make."

"That's it?"

"They're great time fillers between runs, and the materials aren't all that expensive. We even make patchwork ones, which are fun since they're made out of scraps from other production runs; those are no-cost except for manufacturing, and you wouldn't believe the number of people we've taught to make clothes because they wanted a pair of comfortable slippers. You can make your own if you'd like."

"Please," I whispered with wide eyes.

"This is part of why I needed to hire her, Chris."

"So, I see. Do you make those slippers for men?"

"Of course. She can practice making pairs for both of you."

"Is there a reason you don't sell them to the public?" I asked.

"I am a jealous mother of my slippers. So, if you want the slippers, you have to keep the woman, Chris. I've held them back because they're a great employee perk, and I'd rather not turn one of their perks into a money-making gimmick."

I doubted I'd ever understand how the woman operated, but I liked how she put people before herself or her company's profits. "Just so you know, you're really crazy, but I find myself agreeing that you're the good kind of crazy."

"Aren't you laying it on a bit thick, Juliette?" Christopher asked.

"That depends. Did it work?"

Christopher raised a hand and rested his fingertips to his temple before sighing. "Unfortunately, yes."

"Then I didn't lay it on too thick. Pick your first bag. The faster I'm done checking over the suits, the sooner I can leave. Then you two can discuss how you'll proceed moving forward. I really hope I get to plan a Halloween wedding. Weddings beat the costume parties, but nothing beats a wedding that's also a costume party."

"How about a Halloween engagement party instead?" Christopher suggested. "I would rather not force Lee into making any sort of major decision like that without having plenty of time to think it through. I'd also like time to think it through as well."

I wondered how the hell a rich, considerate bachelor had stayed a bachelor for so long. "Please don't be offended I'm asking this, but why are you still single?"

"I have the same question about you."

"Apparently, Jonas has cornered the market on boyfriends, stealing my share of them. He has several, I have none."

"His boyfriends aren't interested in women."

"While that's true, he's much better at attracting men than I am. I'm artsy and, until this point, had a dead-end job in retail. I've found that has killed most of my prospects."

Christopher's brow was at high risk of being stuck in the upright position, and he gestured to his penthouse walls. "I seem to be single due to my artsy tendencies as well."

"I don't understand," I confessed.

"I'd rather go to an art gallery or auction than shoe shopping. It seems many of the women I've met would rather go shoe shopping than to an art gallery."

"I'm surrounded by shoes all day. Please don't take me shoe shopping."

"Hey," Juliette protested.

We both glared at her.

"I like shoes."

"You're a fashion designer, Juliette. You're supposed to like shoes. However, that's no reason to make shoes the star of one's evening life." Christopher maintained his glare, and to my amazement, Juliette threw her hands up in the air.

"I think you won that round, Christopher."

"I do enjoy every time I win against her, and my victory is all the sweeter, as she has already committed to dressing me in her finest suits. I have no idea why, but I'm no fool. If she wants to dress me in her suits, so be it. I'm just not going to think about how much I'll owe her when I'm finished. And no, Juliette, if you don't bill me fairly, I'll go to your billing department and make sure it's sorted properly."

"Cruel and unusual punishment is unconstitutional."

"I've purchased your clothes before, Juliette. You may be able to trick Lee, but you can't trick me. And you, sly woman that you are, know I'm on your waitlist for new suits. All you're doing is fulfilling your contract early rather than making me wait."

I decided it didn't matter if I understood Juliette Carter or not; she needed babysitters before she did something everyone, except her, would regret. With that in mind, I could approach my new job aware she needed help moderating her generosity.

I could do that.

"It did help I already had these pulled aside for you," the woman confessed. "I am an opportunist, and I will not say no to this opportunity."

"I'm still paying for the clothes."

"Why does everyone insist they pay me while I'm busy trying to arrange their marriage?"

"Do I really have to explain this to you?"

"No, no. That's all right. I've heard it before. Apparently, I only try to marry off good people to each other, and good people pay their bills, which makes them good clients. It's not my fault!"

"Did you take your medications today, Juliette?"

"I would answer that, except I really don't know. Probably not," she admitted. "I had to go rescue Lee, and rescue missions are more important than the stupid pills."

"The pills aren't stupid, Juliette. We've talked about this before. You need the pills because your brain is broken, and the pills make your brain not broken. What did you do to help Felicity forget your pills?"

"I didn't do anything to help her forget. I just left the office to rescue Lee; it's not like I did it on purpose."

"Lee, would you mind keeping Juliette amused while I call and find out who has her medications and if she's taken them? The world might end if she's missed a dose."

Juliette sulked, and I wondered if she had missed a dose. If she had, why hadn't everyone at the office mentioned something? Then, with growing dismay, I realized they had discussed her medications. Had it been a hint? I struggled with the possibilities, including accepting she seemed fine enough, and it wasn't worth creating a fuss when she wasn't behaving distressed or causing anyone real harm. "I can do that. What should I do with her?"

"Introduce her to the zombie game and show her the beer bottle. That should do the trick."

I snagged the older woman's arm and dragged her to Christopher's entertainment room, wondering what the hell I'd gotten myself into.

TWELVE

That's the look of a minion about to get uppity with me.

JULIETTE LOVED everything about the broken beer bottle, and I didn't need to play the game to keep her amused. Watching her dish out violence to the undead provided enough entertainment, and while I killed any zombie stupid enough to approach my character, I left her the lion's share.

It took Christopher a rather long time to join us in his entertainment room. "She missed a dose, and her husband will be over in about an hour with it."

"An hour?" Juliette abandoned her controller and hopped to her feet. "But you haven't tried on your suits yet!"

"You have an hour you can dress me up, but that's it. Also, I think your husband is about to have a meltdown."

"He doesn't have meltdowns."

"He most certainly does when he's worried about you because you forgot your medications."

"Is this normal, Christopher?"

"It happens. She's come over off her medications a few times this year so far. I'm willing to bet Juliette gave Felicity new duties when Felicity should only be worrying about Juliette."

"Felicity is wasted doing what she does. She has a good eye, and she's been working on a client's wardrobe. She hit it off with a difficult client, and she's on the schedule." Juliette sighed. "I'm going to get yelled at again."

"Maybe we should tell Naomi?" Naomi seemed like the person to talk to.

"I don't know Naomi," Christopher admitted.

"She's one of my Human Resources minions."

"I'll make the calls, which will take me five minutes, then you'll get me for an hour." Christopher left the room, and I narrowed my eyes, crossed my arms, and tapped my foot.

"I recognize that look. That's the look of a minion about to get uppity with me."

"You deserve to be healthy and happy, too. I know medications are a pain in the ass and hard, but you need to take them. You have a phone. Set alarms to help make sure you take them on time. You hurt yourself most of all when you don't take them, so you really need to take them."

"I left them at the office when I went to meet you," she admitted.

"Then you need to make a checklist of everything that needs to leave the office with you, and your medications need to be on that list."

"You've managed medications before."

"We all had to help my father, especially near the end of his life. Those medications are important, and I don't care what anyone else says, but you need them for a reason, and if your body doesn't produce whatever the hell chemical you need, it's fine that it comes out of a bottle."

"People get so damned judgmental about it."

"That sounds like a *them* problem and not a *you* problem. Also, is an hour enough time for him to try on those suits?"

"Probably, assuming you don't drool all over him each time he struts for us."

"Is he going to strut?"

"I hope so. He's quite handsome in a suit, and watching handsome men show off is one of the perks of my job. He's a quick changer, and he trusts me to do my job, so he won't dawdle unless you're drooling, then he'll dawdle because he will want to impress you. He struggles with the basics."

"He does? He seems like he's doing quite well for himself."

"Yes, but he hasn't figured out how to get you to date him without help. A lot of help."

I shrugged. "Honestly, given a week, I would've wanted to see his paintings again, and then I would've asked Jonas to arrange a coffee date so I could admire the artwork and play that damned zombie game."

"See? I spared you a week of anguish. Now, come along before he gets impatient because there are other things he'd rather be doing than trying on clothes."

I wondered what those other things might be, but rather than ask, I decided I'd wait and find out for myself.

CHRISTOPHER DIDN'T NEED to strut. Walking into the room while wearing a suit was sufficient to capture my attention. To keep from making a complete fool out of myself, I admired his paintings while stealing peeks at him.

I liked him in black suits the best, although Juliette dressed him in one gray one that almost convinced me otherwise.

"Which one do you want him to wear tonight?" Juliette asked. "I bet I can steal the rest of his clothes."

"You're not stealing his clothes, Juliette. He should wear whatever he wants. All of the suits are a good look on him."

"Of course all of the suits look good on him. I designed them. I do not design a bad suit. What color shirts did you like best?"

"The pale blue with the gray, and white or cream with the black. The others aren't bad, but I guess I prefer the classic look," I replied.

"Considering your taste in art, there's a reason for that, I suppose. I could use him to experiment with period wear."

"No codpieces," I announced. "I don't care if they're correct for the period, but I'm drawing a line there. No. I won't have you torturing Christopher with a codpiece."

Christopher laughed. "I have spent an unfortunate number of hours wondering why men wore codpieces. I can't tell if it's a matter of ego, if their trousers lacked a crotch, or what other motivation they had for doing such a thing."

"I'm sure some historian figured it out, but I'm happier just not knowing."

"I agree."

The doorbell rang, and Christopher, dressed in the last black suit of Juliette's collection, went to answer it. He chuckled and let an older gentleman in. "Your wife has mostly behaved herself."

"Juliette, I swear, you do this to cut years off my life sometimes. What have you done now?"

Juliette pointed at me. "Isn't she beautiful?"

"That's a trick question, and I'm not answering it. Also, that would be the young lady you swooned against at the

Halloween party. I have received so many pictures and videos of that incident my phone is going to run out of space. I apologize for her, miss."

"Lee. Please take her home before she steals the little clothes I have left." I gestured to the dress. "Which is this, because she already stole everything else."

"Juliette, again?"

"I'm helping them discover their chemistry!"

"Juliette, they're adults. They don't need chemistry lessons."

"They most certainly do need chemistry lessons leading to marriage. Look at them. They're perfect together. They complement each other. Anyway, my mission here is done. I've got them living together."

Juliette's husband sighed. "I'm so sorry for this, Chris."

"Lee recommended Naomi as someone to talk to; Juliette's bumping her personal assistant to a different department again."

"Tattler!" Juliette stomped a foot.

Juliette's husband snagged her by the back of her neck and dragged her out the door. "I'll give Naomi a call. Thank you for watching her."

"Traitors, all of you!"

Before I could hear any more of Juliette's rant, Christopher closed the door. Then he locked it. And, because he could, he engaged the deadbolt. "That might keep her out."

"Should I be worried?"

"Don't be. He's used to Juliette's insanity. Mr. Carter is usually retrieving her several times a week. Don't tell anyone I said this, but he loves it. It gets him out of his home or office, and she keeps life interesting. But he will call Naomi because while she's fine tonight, she might not be fine another night."

"I've had a lot of people warning me about her medications tonight. Why?"

"I found out because she had an episode during my first fitting. After that, it spread around because a lot of people like her, and nobody knows how to handle her during an anxiety attack. She almost never has them when she's on her medications. And as for her other problems, when her attention span is shot, she forgets the basics, like looking each way down the street before crossing. That's actually more of a problem than her anxiety. A few years back, she got hit by a car because she got distracted while crossing the street. Fortunately, she emerged with a few scrapes and a sprained wrist, but now everyone's on guard about it."

"I had no idea that could be an issue," I admitted.

"It's different for everyone. Usually, she just lacks an attention span and gets hyperactive. I don't have a problem with it, and most don't, but it's a coin toss if she's able to work, and then she gets anxiety attacks because she wasn't able to work when she needed to, and that's where the trouble comes in."

"I'm really sorry you got dragged into this."

"I'm not. Do you have any idea how hard it is to find someone actually willing to talk to me about my paintings?"

"Apparently not. I figured a lot of rich people did things like talk about art."

"They prefer to talk about their latest work acquisitions or cars."

Ew. I wrinkled my nose at that. "I'd rather get stung by a bee, and I'm allergic."

"How allergic?"

"Allergic enough that I need to go to the hospital but not allergic enough that I need to carry allergy pens. It takes about an hour before I start going into anaphylactic shock. That's a good thing, as I can't afford the allergy pens."

"You can afford the allergy pens now. What do you do if you get stung?"

"I head to the nearest hospital, wait around in the emergency room while they tell me it's not that bad and I'll be fine. Then, when I can't breathe, they realize I was telling the truth and they deal with it."

Christopher closed his eyes, bowed his head, and sighed. "You're like Juliette, but with allergies."

"That seems like a fair and warranted statement."

"Okay. I have a friend who is a doctor, and he lives near where I have to run an errand to tonight. We'll stop somewhere on the way to get you clothes, so you're not forced to wear a Carter dress, if that's all right with you?"

"That's all right with me. I'm really sorry for making a mess of your evening plans."

"The only thing I've missed was my shower, but it'll be fine. I'll get changed, and then we'll go. If you'd like, you can try on a pair of my sweats. You'll swim in them, but it might be better than going into a twenty-four-hour store dressed up like that."

"Do you have a safe I can put the jewelry in?"

"I was thinking you could still wear those. They're beautiful on you, and they were worth every penny spent."

My cheeks warmed. "Thank you. They are lovely. No one has ever bought something like this for me before."

"That's why I did it. Jonas told me a little about you, and I thought you deserved something special. That was all I could get on short notice, especially after hearing he'd made a wager with you about playing in the park. You're tenacious, and I regret I hadn't gotten something better for you after hearing you play."

"Something better?" I lifted my hand and touched the necklace, my eyes widening. "You got me two paintings and this. How could it get better?"

"I haven't figured that out yet, but it's on my list of things to do in the near future. Juliette is right, though. I'm awkward and rather useless at meeting women. I was getting a play by play from a few of her minions, as they didn't want me to be caught off guard."

"You came to the door shirtless on purpose?"

"As a matter of fact, yes. I figured if you didn't run away screaming, that would be a good sign, and I hoped to embarrass Juliette. It turns out I encouraged her instead. Oh, well. That said, I had really meant to take a quick shower before you showed up. I thought I'd have a few extra minutes."

"You were trying to plan the dripping wet and shirtless look, then?"

"Guilty as charged. I figured if it worked on television, it might work in real life."

"We can experiment later with the dripping wet and shirtless look. Me? I'll spare you. I look like a creature from a horror flick when my hair gets wet and dangles in my face. It's thick, it makes a mess, and it takes forever to dry. There is absolutely nothing sexy about my hair when wet."

"I may be awkward, but I have a sister, and I used to brush her hair growing up. Please don't tell her this, but I actually enjoyed my hair-brushing duties. Now my sister is a demon in disguise out to marry me, too."

"You prefer Juliette's marrying ploys over your sister's I

take it?" I hoped so, considering my presence in his penthouse.

"The last time my sister attempted such a ploy, she tried to hook me up with a porn star. While I'm not about to judge a woman for working in pornography, I don't want to be in a relationship with someone who has sex with other men and women as part of her career. Jonas wouldn't mind that sort of thing, but I do. That was my last blind date. Honestly, I've been hiding from my sister ever since."

"Do you need to be rescued from your sister?"

"Now that you mention it, yes."

I regarded the dress I wore with a frown. "Well, I'm dressed appropriately. So are you. Is a meeting with your sister possible?"

"My errand, ironically, involves my sister. It's something we've done together since high school, so I see her multiple times a week."

"I guess that means we're not dressed appropriately for whatever you're doing, then."

"Yeah, we need to be dressed casually."

"I feel like we should call Juliette back and ask for help."

"She would go overboard, we'd be late, and there's a store down the street from our destination if you're okay with wearing my sweats until we get there."

Why not? What was a little embarrassment? I'd already been seen with Clarissa while she'd worn an inflatable dinosaur costume. "Bring me your sweats and a belt of some sort. A sash from a bathrobe will work if you have one. Are you really sure you want me to wear the jewelry?"

"Beautiful things are meant to be worn and seen, and on you, it's a piece of art. But I do have to admit, they pale in comparison to those pearls you were wearing in the park. They suited you."

"They're cheap."

"So was the winter landscape painting you like so much. Cheap isn't a word for bad, Lee. I like expensive paintings—that's true—but I like cheap ones if they're beautiful. I care less about the name on the canvas and more about the art, anyway."

"Can I ask how much a cheap painting is? Because the winter one is my favorite."

Christopher smiled. "I heard. There's a picture of you clutching it rather possessively. Anyway, the canvas was about thirty dollars, and I probably spent forty dollars on the paint. In retrospect, I wish I'd used a better canvas."

My eyes widened, and my mouth dropped open. I pointed at him and spluttered. When my tongue finally did what I wanted it to, I blurted, "You painted that?"

"I did. You play the harp, I paint. Maybe sometime soon, you'll play the harp while I paint. I think Juliette's right, though. We do complement each other. To be honest, I sent the winter landscape on impulse. I was worried you wouldn't like it since it isn't really a Renaissance piece."

"But it's beautiful. Of course I love it. You really painted it?"

"I don't really look like a painter, do I?"

"I will admit, I didn't check under your nails for paint."

"I'm very careful to keep my painting a dirty secret. I usually wear gloves to keep my hands from being stained."

"That's incredible. Do you paint here?"

"I have a room that is locked and closed off just for painting. It's the room with the entry to the balcony, and I keep my painting supplies out of view of the window—or keep the curtains closed."

"I want to watch you paint."

He grinned. "I don't have any errands tomorrow night, so you can watch me to your heart's content. I usually paint for two or three hours in the evening when I don't have to run any errands. I'll just wait until you get here before I start."

"I will rescue my harp from Juliette tomorrow," I swore. "I can play and watch you paint at the same time. I think."

"And even if you can't, you can play for me later. I wouldn't want you to hurt your fingers, and I saw how you'd winced at the park after playing for a while. In the next few weeks, I might do a restoration, and I like things quiet when I'm doing a restoration."

"You do restoration work?"

Christopher pointed at one of the flower paintings on the wall. "I bought that one for less than ten dollars at an estate sale."

"It's beautiful."

"It's worth over a hundred thousand dollars now that it isn't covered in a layer of filth and I've finished some basic restoration work on it. I'm picky about my paintings, so I had it evaluated both before and after restoration. The people running the estate sale had no idea what they had. I have seven other paintings from the estate sale, but I haven't had time to do more than to put them in my painting room while I try to figure out what they are. They're in awful condition. My appraiser laughed at me when I showed him the photographs and told me to come back after I got the grime off them. Once I have them cleaned, I'll take them in to see what I have. I'm not even sure the one can be restored. While the canvas isn't torn, it's not in good shape."

"Is there anything you can't do?"

"A lot, including build healthy relationships with women. The instant they find out I'm obsessed with classical art, they run the other way."

"That's stupid. I was trying to think about ways to pressure you into inviting me back."

"Using me for my paintings?"

"Definitely." I pointed at his prized Leonardo da Vinci sketch. "I want coffee or tea dates underneath that. We can sit on the floor and marvel at its beauty."

"I'm pretty sure I can manage that."

"It might have to be our morning ritual. We get up, make coffee or tea, and come in here to admire the artwork while we wake up."

"I have an entire parlor and a dining room, both of which are decorated with paintings."

"We can start here and move that way eventually. There has to be at least two or three months of admiration in your entry alone."

Christopher checked his watch. "Hold that thought until later tonight. If we don't leave soon, we'll be late for everything. I expect we're going to need an hour at the store to pick up all the basics for you, and we'll make some time to do more shopping tomorrow."

"Jonas bought me a laptop for Christmas, and I am happy to order everything online. I assume your fancy penthouse allows for delivery?"

Christopher laughed. "And the guys downstairs will hold packages and help carry them up, too. Delivery works. I'll make sure they know you're living here, so you're added to the list of people allowed free access to the building. Don't tell Juliette this, but the only reason she got away with what she did was because I'd called downstairs to let them know she was coming and was up to her usual tricks."

"You played her, and she doesn't even have a clue."

"Isn't it great?"

It was, which made me laugh. "I think you won this round."

"I know I did."

CHRISTOPHER LOANED me the sash of his bathrobe and a pair of sweats, which I swam in but refused to complain. He couldn't prevent the walk to the elevator or down to the garage, but the security people didn't spare us more than a glance before returning to work, and no one else was around.

He owned a sports car and an SUV, and he gave his fancy, expensive car the kind of glare I planned to reserve for rats.

"I don't know what your car did to you, but if I were it, I'd be worried."

"It is ten years old, and its engine is on its way out the door. It starts, barely. I'll have to have it towed to a shop. I got it because I liked this specific car in that specific year. I made an error of judgment. It's a pain in my ass. I keep thinking I should replace it, but then a new painting I want crosses my path, and I have to pick between the car or the painting. Without exception, I choose the painting. Or, as is the case this week, some other worthwhile investment."

As he'd asked, I still wore the diamond and ruby jewelry. I still didn't understand why he'd gotten them for me, but I'd solve the mystery one day, even if I had to ask him. For the moment, I'd do my best to pretend they were made of glass rather than precious stones.

His vehicle issues would provide a good distraction for a little while. "I know nothing about cars, so I'll just say the SUV is probably more sensible. It can also hold more paintings and paint supplies. It can also hold my harp."

"I like your priorities. The last time I brought a woman down to my spots, she gave my car the glare because it wasn't fancy enough."

"That's never a good sign."

"No, it's really not. I guess I should confess I'd installed cameras all throughout my penthouse since I was letting people in without me being able to supervise everyone. I may have reviewed the images you were in. Your eyes lit up when you saw my artwork. You even got Jonas to tag along while you admired everything. He looked like he wanted to jump off my balcony by the time he got you down to the entertainment room."

"Art is so not his thing, the poor fool."

"Don't tell Juliette this, but I owe her a favor or three for bringing you back. I wasn't sure how I was going to approach you."

"For coffee, as we'd discussed."

"Would that have actually worked?"

"As a matter of fact, yes. But don't worry. Even if you hadn't asked for coffee, I would've concocted reasons to visit you. Your art collection is only one of your lures."

"Can I ask what the other lures are?"

I considered, but then I shook my head. "I'm sure you will figure them out soon enough. I wouldn't want to bereave you of a chance to learn my secrets."

"I feel I should warn you I can be quite competitive."

Good. "It's important for relationships to have some spice."

"To go with your morning cup of chai?"

"Honestly, I have no idea how to make chai."

"I do."

"Does Juliette know this?"

"Surprisingly, yes. She's been over a lot during the initial fittings; she came to me since I live so close to her office. I usually make it from scratch. Working with spices is like working with paints for me. I find it relaxing. I am also a bit of a snob, so all of my teas are loose-leaf. I do have bags you can put the tea in if you must."

"Tea comes as loose-leaf?"

Christopher unlocked the SUV. "Get in. I see I have a lot of work to do. Also, I'll pay for everything you get tonight, and if you're unhappy because you like being independent, you can pay me back after you get your bonus from Juliette. I'll probably give her the receipt just to watch her meltdown. The thought of one of her employees going to Walmart for clothing will drive her crazy."

"She was going to take me to thrift stores," I confessed, climbing in and buckling my seatbelt. "That's usually my speed."

Christopher got into the SUV, and he took his time getting settled, buckling in, and starting the engine. "I'd be game, but most of them are already closed for the night or closing, so I have to go with what's open."

"Walmart will have everything in one place. I'm good to go, but I don't want to spend an hour in Walmart. That's like visiting hell and being expected to stay." I dug out my new phone, scrolled through the available apps, and found one that let me create a list. "You drive, I will make a list. I will then conquer the list in as expedient a fashion as possible."

"There's a McDonald's inside we can have for dinner. Not great cuisine, but we won't get a chance to eat until after, so I recommend we grab something."

"I like their salads."

"Me too, actually. It's one of my guilty indulgences."

"I think we have the important bases covered. What's wrong with you?" I asked.

"Nothing. I'm male perfection."

I laughed. "Jonas must be so sad you're not gay."

"In his eyes, that is my greatest flaw. I'm unavailable for his enjoyment. And my art. For some reason, he's just not a fan."

"He needs more help than even doctors can provide."

"That's what I thought, but when I suggested that, he laughed at me. One day, he might learn."

"I find that highly improbable. This is Jonas we're talking about."

"You're right. Just be glad we're talking about Jonas and not Clarissa." Christopher regarded me with a raised brow. "You do know Clarissa is going to flip, right?"

"She is? Why?"

"I told her, to her face, that I like my crazy to be cultured."

I covered my mouth with my hand in a futile effort to keep from laughing. "She must hate you."

"I'm tempted to text her that I have you in my custody and have no intention of releasing you anytime soon. It would be enjoyable for one of us. By that, I mean me."

"She might come over wearing an inflatable dinosaur costume."

"I heard about that. Honestly, I'd pay good money for that

sort of entertainment. I'll text her, tell her when I'm dragging you back to my domain, and we can have some fun at her expense for a change."

"Rather than at mine?"

"Yep."

"I'm viewing the Tiffany ring as the requirement met for the ring, the Halloween engagement party as the requirement for a serious relationship, and we'll have to talk about future plans."

"Your list of requirements for indulging in sharing someone else's bed?"

"Precisely."

"I like children, but I'm up in the air on if I want to adopt. I've been leaning towards adoption, as I see zero need for my child to share my genes. That, plus I can't imagine asking a woman to undergo that sort of discomfort when there are plenty of kids who need a family. I haven't put in any serious thought beyond that, as I've been working fairly long hours and running errands. I'll have to change my schedule."

"I haven't thought about children at all, as I've never been able to afford them."

"I have no aspirations of moving, honestly. I've spent most of my excess money paying my mortgage off early, and I've been working overtime to make sure the only bill for my penthouse is maintenance fees and property tax. I'm about a year out from paying it off entirely, so I'd like to wait on any big moves until then."

"Thus, the engagement party in a year?"

"No, that was for the reasons I said. We both deserve to take our time thinking about it and getting to know each other better. I'm game for a year trial living under the same roof and figuring out how we tick. For some reason, I think we'll be fine."

I thought he was right, too. "Is there space for a proper full-sized harp?"

"I can make space. If you want a full-sized harp for the painting room, we can do that. I also have room in the main parlor for one. I see no reason you can't have two full-sized harps. It's a big penthouse, so we can arrange it for what works with us. I'm not going to say no if you want harps. I have a bedroom that we can convert into a music room for you, but I'm not sure about its acoustics. I'll hire a contractor to go through the extra bedrooms and figure out which one is best. I might have the painting room redone at the same time. It could use some work. I've made a mess of it."

"You're painting in there. You're supposed to make a mess of it."

"Let's just say you will want a cheaper harp in that room because it will get paint on it. I do splash therapy sometimes."

"Splash therapy? What's that?"

"I buy cheap acrylics, water them down, and fling them at the canvas. Aggressively. It's messy. I cover the works in process with loose canvas, too. I've actually made some interesting pieces that way. Once, I cleared out all of my paintings, put a canvas down on the floor, and rolled on it while covered in paint."

"That sounds amazing. That also sounds like something I could do. Easily. While dressed in an inflatable dinosaur costume."

Christopher's eyes widened. "We're going to do that, and when we're done, we're going to sell it."

"We are?"

"People love crazy art, Lee. And I'm going to record you while you roll around on the canvas and turn it into art. And so you don't feel left out, I'll join you, also dressed in an inflatable dinosaur costume. We can make new ones every now and then while wearing new costumes."

"Think Juliette will flip if I alter another perfect black dress, turn it into a witch's costume, dress you up as a black cat, and roll around in paint and force her to watch it?"

"Just don't do it to the black dress you wore tonight. I'll beg, just don't do it to that dress. I really will beg but spare the dress."

"Like it, do you?"

"On you, it's perfection. I'll try to find a replacement for your ruined dress and get everything you need to recreate it. I have pictures if you need to see them for reference. It's a Prada?"

"It used to be. It's now a rats' nest."

"I'll contact Prada and ask if they can get a new one sent over in your size. I'm more than happy to replace the dress, especially as you intend to use it to teach Juliette a lesson."

I swallowed my pride, straightened my shoulders, and asked, "Can you ask for two? It really was the perfect dress. I'll pay you back for it."

"Consider the second one a Christmas present. I don't do the Christmas present thing all that well, so you'll have to tell me what you want; otherwise, you're getting art."

"How tragic, to receive art for Christmas? Whatever will I do?"

He laughed. "Yeah, for some reason, I didn't think you'd mind."

"I've never been able to afford much in the way of Christmas presents before, so expect me to go overboard."

"However will I cope? If you feel you must pay rent, I'll apply it to the mortgage, and once there's no mortgage, it will go into a retirement fund or to pay the property taxes. I do not expect the woman living with me to pay any rent, but I also refuse to be one of those men who refuse to accept help. It's a partnership."

"I'm glad we don't have to have that fight. My income is based on twenty percent going to rent, so I will take twenty percent of my paycheck and apply it to the mortgage, property taxes, or a savings account."

"Retirement account."

I frowned. "Is there a difference?"

"Yes, there are. I'll explain it when we get to that point. If there's one thing in this life I'm good at, it's handling money."

"Painting. You're definitely better at painting."

"I think you're biased."

"Yes, I am. Deal."

He chuckled, backed the SUV out of its spot, and eased through the maze of luxury vehicles in the parking garage. "Okay. I'll deal and I'll even enjoy it."

I thought I would, too. To make sure we wasted as little time in Walmart as possible, I made my shopping list and wondered what the future would hold.

THIRTEEN

It's only partially her fault; she stole
my clothes.

UNLIKE MOST BEES AND WASPS, some species of hornets came out at night to play, and someone had disturbed a nest at the Secaucus Walmart in New Jersey.

Two stings, three hornet assassinations courtesy of Christopher, and one hospital trip later, I became the not-so-proud owner of a medical bill, two allergy pens, and a drug-induced stupor. Then, because I couldn't handle making Christopher late for his errand, we had our first spat over whether he should stay with me while the doctors waited to confirm my condition wouldn't worsen.

If I hadn't told him about my allergy, things might've worked out a lot differently.

I won the argument, sent him off with a promise I wouldn't be going anywhere for at least six hours, and played on my new phone. It took me two hours to work up the nerve to confess the truth about my allergies to Clarissa, who, as expected, told everyone.

My parents, my second parents, and my best friend

showed up at the hospital while I twiddled my thumbs and waited to see if the hornets would win.

"Since when have you been allergic to bees?" Clarissa shrieked.

"Since birth," my mother announced, and she glared at me. "What do you think you're doing?"

"I didn't mean to play with hornets, Mom. They took over the Walmart, and before we realized someone had disturbed a nest, I got stung."

Clarissa drew in a deep breath and straightened her shoulders. "Where's that bitch?"

"Bitch? Which bitch?" I asked.

"Juliette Carter. This is her fault," Clarissa snarled.

"Actually, it's really not. Her husband took her home. Well, it's only partially her fault; she stole my clothes."

"That explains why you're wearing sweats. But whose sweats are those?" my mother frowned. "Are they hospital sweats?"

"No. They're Christopher's. Frankly, I'm amazed they didn't put me in one of those gowns. Maybe that comes if they have to do more than give me a needle or two. I think they gave me every antihistamine on the planet, Mom."

"That's better than a tube down your throat. How long did it take you to get to the hospital this time?"

"About ten minutes. Christopher had to kill a hornet that got into the SUV. He parked right near the disturbed nest. It was an ambush."

Clarissa scowled. "Why is Christopher driving you around, anyway?"

"I'm living with him now. Juliette dropped me off and expected me to stay. Upon some careful consideration and unlimited access to his artwork for my admiration, I accepted her decision with no complaints. Christopher didn't seem to mind having someone who likes his art around, so we decided it was a mutually beneficial arrangement. Anyway, he needed to run an errand, and I needed clothes, and that was the nearest Walmart."

"Why are you buying clothes at Walmart?"

"Because it will upset Juliette, duh. That, plus I didn't have a lot of things." I regarded my shopping list with a resigned sigh. "I had a good list and everything."

Second Dad held out his hand. "Give me the list, and I will buy everything. I'll take your dad with me, and we'll get out of your hair while the women try to teach you the importance of leaving bees and their kin alone."

"Winged ass assassins," I muttered. I tapped at the screen until I figured out how to email a copy of the list, and I sent it to Dad. "Dad, I just emailed you the list."

"My, my. Someone has joined the modern times. I'm so proud of you."

Wow. Dad's sarcasm skills had gone up a level, and I stared at him with wide eyes. "I'm sorry. I didn't mean to play with the hornets. They ambushed me. They're *evil*. Evil winged ass assassins. I think Christopher got stung, too, but he isn't allergic."

I suspected Christopher had gotten stung more times than me trying to keep me from getting stung in the first place, but he had refused to worry about it.

Damned people who lacked bee allergies, treating their stings as a general nuisance rather than a nightmare. I didn't look forward to having to dish out six hundred for the allergy pens, as my prescription plan was less than ideal.

All mine did was cover the minimums.

At the rate I was going, my hiring bonus would be gone before I got a chance to buy anything.

Both of my dads glared at me, and in a unified front, they left the hospital room armed with my shopping list. That left my mothers, who wore matching expressions of disgust.

"What? It's not my fault hornets are evil winged ass assassins who hunt at night. It's definitely not my fault someone had disturbed their nest prior to our arrival."

My mother sighed. "I'm more amazed you didn't procrastinate before going to the hospital."

"I'd told Christopher about my allergy."

"You told him, but you hadn't told *me*?" Clarissa turned her back to me and sniffled. "I am planning revenge."

"And I'm planning on replacing my Prada, perfecting it again, and destroying it on purpose to get back at Juliette Carter."

Silence.

"What? Is it that unbelievable?"

"Yes," everyone replied.

I shrugged. "There'll be a video, too. I'll enjoy it. It's her punishment for forcing me to work for her."

"You're...working for Juliette Carter?" my mother asked. "The fashion designer? That Juliette Carter?"

"You knew Shirley was scheming with that devil. Juliette left a ransom note in my bras. You laughed about it and thought it might be nice having a third woman helping to raise your daughter."

I giggled at the thought of my mothers bickering in my second mother's living room and planning to add a third mother to the mix while it was decorated with lingerie. "I wasn't scheming. I was cooperating. There is a difference.

Also, I'm not sure I want to be adopted by Juliette. She's a little crazy, Mom. But in a good way."

My second mother grunted. "She hung my bras all over my living room and left a ransom note."

"I think she transferred my person to Christopher, so you'll have to take that up with him."

"Where is this Christopher?" my mother demanded.

According to my mother's tone, she wouldn't leave Christopher alive when she was finished with him. "He's running an important errand. I forced him to leave so he could attend to his errand. He was very upset with me over being evicted. It's not like having him stand around doing nothing will change anything, so he gets his errand done, and only one of us has to sit around and wait to see if I up and die from the latest winged ass assassination attempt."

"Could you please stop calling it that? Take this seriously."

"Explain how it wasn't a winged ass assassination attempted," I countered.

Sometimes, I truly adored the sound of silence.

"There's only one thing left for us to do. We must wait for Christopher. He can explain everything."

"I wish you the best of luck, Clarissa. I don't think he has any more of an idea of what's going on than I do. But it's okay. I get to live with pretty pieces of art. That's worth being stung by a winged ass assassin or two."

"You're impossible," my mother grumbled, and like everyone else visiting me, she settled in to wait.

It was going to be a long night.

FIVE HOURS AFTER LEAVING, Christopher showed up with Sophia in tow, and we pointed at each other.

"*You're* Christopher's sister?"

"*You're* his girlfriend?"

I could understand why Sophia would be incredulous. I wasn't the type to date or do anything interesting, including date someone so far out of my league. Scratching my head, I marveled at how small the world could be. "*You* tried to set *him* up with a porn star?"

"Of all the things to bring up, you had to bring up that?" Sophia turned onto her brother and jabbed him in the chest. "And you're making off with one of *my* friends?"

"In my defense, I had no idea you two knew each other. I knew you knew Clarissa, but that was inevitable since I'm friends with Jonas. I just hadn't realized you were friend friends with Clarissa."

"Friend friends?" Clarissa frowned, and her brow furrowed. "I should be offended by that, but you make a good point. Sophia is one of the few I trust to not be a bitch to Shirley."

"I was all prepared to come here and defend my brother's honor from his new girlfriend, but I can't complain about the girlfriend. This is unfair."

"How about I direct you towards the hornets? They're the real reason I was late tonight. Also, I'm sorry I was late. I didn't want to leave Lee alone, and we were fighting over it, and she didn't want to make me late, but well, I was late."

"Chris, all you had to do was call in that your girlfriend's allergic to bees and got stung. It's not the end of the world if you're late for once in your life. Really."

"I would've stayed here, but she kicked me out, so I wasn't here, *and* I was late," Christopher groused.

I raised my hand. "Question?"

"It's not school, Lee. What is it?" Sophia laughed, shaking her head. "Who am I kidding? You likely have so many questions you don't even know where to start."

"While that's true, what was that errand, anyway? I'm sorry I missed whatever it was."

"We volunteer at a women's shelter not too far away from here. We help out unless there's an incident."

My eyes widened. "An incident?"

"That's when someone needs to leave their situation in a hurry. We work with a non-profit, and we help people leave dangerous situations, especially when there are children involved. The police reach out to us if they get a call, and we handle everything from there. Chris tries to keep openings at his company for those who are fleeing a domestic violence situation. If he doesn't have openings, he usually knows someone who does, so it works out really well. There's usually an incident every night, though we've gotten plenty of mid-day calls. Chris will have one of his employees handle it during the day if he's busy. If he's not, he handles it himself."

I wasn't the only one who stared at Chris. Clarissa spluttered, and she pointed at him. "That is not something the demon Chris I know would do. No, no. You're the demon Chris, who seduces my brother!"

"Just because I'm friends with your brother doesn't mean I'm gay, Clarissa."

"Why else would you be friends with him?"

Wow. I jabbed Clarissa with my elbow. "Despite your brother's acts, he can be nice. He's probably friends with Christopher because they like the same kind of video games, and it's good to be friends with those who are different from you. That, plus Christopher isn't the judgmental bastard type. Jonas probably deals with judgmental bastards all of the time."

"While that's true, I really thought Chris was gay, too."

I stared at her. "Are you insane?"

"Wow. That was mean," Clarissa complained.

"There's nothing gay about Christopher."

My friend scowled. "How would you even know? You just met him!"

Sophia laughed. "He's not gay, Clarissa. I've told you this before."

"He turned down a porn star."

Sophia shrugged. "I was getting desperate. She thought he was hot and wanted to try him out, and well, it's not like he was doing anything about his single situation on his own. It never occurred to me to toss Lee at him."

"Her enjoyment of prissy art should've tipped us off," Clarissa muttered.

"Hey," I complained. "It's not prissy art. It's beautiful art. It just happens Christopher decided to buy all the art I like. That's hardly my fault. I'm an innocent bystander in this entire situation."

"You cut up a Prada for a Halloween costume. You only have yourself to blame for how this turned out," my friend replied.

"I'm going to cut up another Prada, too. Christopher is going to help me get two. One for keeping, one for costuming. Right?"

Christopher grinned and nodded. "It'll be fun. I'm particularly looking forward to dumping paint all over you and tossing you on the canvas to see what happens."

Sophia scowled. "You are not doing that to her."

"It was her idea."

"There's going to be a video," I added.

"Well, shit. They're on the same page. This is even worse than I feared." Sophia pointed at Clarissa. "You corrupted them!"

"I corrupted them? I didn't even know they were interested in each other until she texted me that she was stuck in the hospital waiting to find out if the winged ass assassins were going to actually kill her off this time. Also, I'm so mad at you over that, Lee. You cut years off my life. Why didn't you tell me you're allergic to bees?"

"It wasn't an issue before."

"Being allergic to bees is always an issue."

"I'm sorry I didn't tell you I was allergic to bees. It's not like I have issues with bees often."

My mother raised a brow. "Only three or four times a year. Then you call me and complain about your latest misadventure requiring a trip to urgent care, resulting in a medical bill you pay off twenty dollars at a time because you can't afford them."

Busted. "It's not my fault the medical care system is stupid, my insurance doesn't cover everything, and they're willing to do payment plans. And after the first visit of the year, I hit my cap and I don't have to worry about it. I've already hit cap this year."

"Shirley," my mother warned.

"I see your financial situation is even worse than I thought," Christopher said, shaking his head and laughing. "Make sure Juliette knows you have medical bills. She hates medical bills with a passion. She'll also want to know you're allergic to bees."

"As long as she isn't keeping bees in her building, I should be fine. It's not like I go out of my way to find bees."

"Getting stung three or four times a year is going out of your way to find bees. Until tonight, I'd gone years without being stung by anything."

Well, shit. "I just have bad luck and like flowers. Winged ass assassins like flowers, too."

"Please be careful around anything that might sting you."

"I can do that."

Christopher turned to Clarissa and narrowed his eyes. When he didn't say a word, my friend blurted, "It wasn't me!"

"Actually, it probably was you," Sophia replied. "All of this is probably your fault. Particularly, it was you and that awful dinosaur costume. You broke Lee with it. I saw the pictures. Lee looked absolutely crestfallen and traumatized. I knew I should've gone to that party if only to rescue her from you. Now you've corrupted her into doing what with my brother?"

"Nothing yet," Christopher replied. "I haven't done anything with Lee yet, except invite her to stay in my home. I was a gentleman."

I covered my mouth so I wouldn't laugh. Somehow, I kept my amusement to myself.

"The keyword here is yet." According to Sophia's expression, she didn't trust her brother at all.

"We're adults, Sophia. We can do whatever we want to each other."

While true, I could understand why Juliette thought Christopher was his own worst enemy. "I'm a willing accomplice in this, Sophia. No worries. That, plus, have you seen his art collection? And I was the one who started it. I used him as a scapegoat to get rid of an idiot. He was quite the gentleman."

I looked forward to future incidents involving his mouth, too.

Sophia huffed, crossed her arms, and wrinkled her nose. "Well, considering he is my brother, I've had the misfortune of hearing about his latest acquisitions, and as I'm a good sister, I visit him so he can show them off to me."

"Misfortune? How is that a *misfortune*? His collection is beautiful. Don't say such horrible things about his art collection."

"Right. You're as art obsessed as he is. We're going to have to keep an eye on the local museums. If you visit together, you might never come out. You'll probably stand around talking about the art until you starve to death."

"Clarissa, you've been teaching Sophia bad habits again."

"I have not. It's Christopher's fault. She came to me already corrupted."

"Why am I being blamed? I didn't do anything."

"This time." Sophia uncrossed her arms and prodded her brother's chest. "Here's the rules. You will take good care of Lee. We will be checking in on her at least once a week, making certain you are taking good care of her. If we find out you are not taking good care of Lee, your sketch gets it."

"Like hell, his sketch gets it!" I waved my fist at Sophia. "Don't punish me. I love that sketch. I will kill you if you do anything to that sketch or any of his art. I will more than kill you. I'll shred your fancy clothes and dump the scraps off of a skyscraper."

Sophia held her hands up in surrender. "Right. You're an art-obsessed freak. Fine. His game console gets it."

"No. I plan on playing that. I have zombies to decapitate with broken beer bottles."

"Well, shit, Lee. What can I do to him, then?"

"Go after his car and mock him ruthlessly over it," I suggested. "Take it away and show up with a better one, thus forcing him to grovel in thanks for being a kind sister."

Christopher's eyes widened. "That's not even fair."

"Perfect. If you are at all mean to Lee, your car's going to get it."

Christopher's expression turned puzzled, and he stared at me in helpless confusion. I shrugged. "You heard your sister. Be nice to me, or that car's going to get it."

"I'm going to need a clear definition of what counts as being mean and counts as being nice. I'm not sure I know what to do."

"I'll just have Lee tell us if you've been mean or nice," Clarissa announced. "Well, Lee?"

"He's definitely been mean, and you should torture that car within an inch of its life. Then you should force him to accept a new one. He's been so mean you should get Juliette to help you, because she, apparently, likes cars. You can stage it at Christmas, so he's forced to cooperate with you."

"Since when have you been so ruthless, Lee?" Clarissa whispered. "That's just *harsh*."

The doctor came in with a nurse, and they checked my vitals before announcing I could be discharged. I managed to evict everyone except Christopher from the room while I handled the paperwork.

I didn't look forward to filling the prescription for my new allergy pens.

Christopher, at my invitation, reviewed my paperwork,

Bat out of Hell

nodding his satisfaction before handing the sheets back. "What was that about with my sister and Clarissa?"

"That was payback for subjecting me to the dinosaur costume. I'm certain your sister encouraged that travesty, so she's fair game. You win, since you don't have to worry about your car, Juliette wins because she enjoys cars, and they lose, as someone who isn't you has to pay for the car, and I know full well that both of those wenches can afford whatever they're planning for revenge. My second parents will probably help, as nobody in that family has any common sense."

"Most people would be upset over their car being trashed by a bunch of angry women, but it seems I'm coming out the clear winner of this situation."

"I know. Isn't it great?"

"Well, one thing's for certain."

"What's for certain?" I asked.

"The future is going to be bright and very, very interesting."

That it was.

About the Author

Bernadette Franklin is a figment of imagination owned and operated by two cats, some plants, and a human.

The human also writes as RJ Blain and Susan Copperfield.

Want to hear from the author when a new book releases? You can sign up at her website (thesneakykittycritic.com). Please note this newsletter is operated by the Furred & Frond Management. Expect to be sassed by a cat. (With guest features of other animals, including dogs.)

A complete list of books written by RJ and her various pen names is available at https://books2read.com/rl/The-Fantasy-Worlds-of-RJ-Blain.

RJ BLAIN suffers from a Moleskine journal obsession, a pen fixation, and a terrible tendency to pun without warning.

When she isn't playing pretend, she likes to think she's a cartographer and a sumi-e painter.

In her spare time, she daydreams about being a spy. Should that fail, her contingency plan involves tying her best of enemies to spinning wheels and quoting James Bond villains until she is satisfied.

RJ also writes as Susan Copperfield and Bernadette Franklin. Visit RJ and her pets (the Management) at thesneakykittycritic.com.

Follow RJ & her alter egos on Bookbub:
RJ Blain
Susan Copperfield
Bernadette Franklin